Angel Of The Morning

The Magic Jukebox, Volume 7

Judith Arnold

Published by Judith Arnold, 2018.

ANGEL OF THE MORNING
The Magic Jukebox: BOOK SEVEN

***

.

***

Chapter One

The view from the back porch was exactly what Dylan wanted.

Actually, it was more of a veranda than a porch, with an overhang casting shade over most of it. Two steps below it lay a curving patio of inlaid brick and stone, complete with a built-in fire pit. Beyond that a grassy slope descended to the beach and the ocean, blue and green and gray, spreading east to meet the horizon.

Behind him, one of the French doors opened and Andrea Simonetti stepped out into the chilly October air. He'd contacted her not long after he'd lost out on *The Angel* and decided he wanted to change everything in his life. Well, not everything, but he definitely wanted to change the ocean. For some reason, the Atlantic resonated more with him than the Pacific. He'd sold his house in California and flown east in search of a new home.

Maybe the move had nothing to do with which coast he lived on, or which ocean he swam in. Maybe it was just that he had memories of his stay in Brogan's Point six years ago. The last time he'd spent time in this town, he'd been hovering on a threshold, about to step across it and into an entirely new life. He'd been a kid with dreams and ambitions, on the cusp of becoming a star.

He couldn't complain about stardom. He loved that his new life had made him wealthy enough that he could afford a house with an ocean view.

But he wanted something more than just a house overlooking the Atlantic Ocean. He wanted something real, something basic. Something far from Hollywood in both distance and atmosphere. If he couldn't have *The Angel*, he'd take Brogan's Point.

Andrea joined him at the porch railing. Her hair barely moved in the brisk breeze rolling up from the beach. She must have shellacked it with several gallons of hair spray. Her make-up was impeccable, the silk scarf around her neck tasteful. Dylan, on the other hand, wore a scuffed

1

leather bomber jacket, ratty jeans, old sneakers, and a Red Sox cap. He'd
taken his sunglasses off during his tour of the house, but he would put
them on again once he was back in public, even though the afternoon
was overcast, the sky a dull gray.

He didn't care about the clouds. He was gazing at the ocean, and
the view was amazing.

"I've got to tell you, Dylan, we don't see many beach-front houses
for sale here," Andrea reminded him. "They tend to get passed down
through families, from one generation to the next. And we're in the
off-season, in terms of real estate transactions. We might get a few more
properties listed next May or June, but if you're determined to buy
now, I'd suggest that you make an offer on this property. You won't
find anything closer to what you're looking for, at least not in Brogan's
Point."

"What was the asking price again?"

"One point nine-five million."

"Tell the sellers I'll pay one-point-five."

"That's a bit low," she warned.

"So they'll make a counter-offer. Let's see where we go with this."
The house needed work, after all. The kitchen and bathrooms hadn't
been updated in at least thirty years, and he was wary about the energy
efficiency of the heating system. The structure was old, a rambling
Victorian on an acre of land which, like the house, cried out for tender
loving care. A low-ball bid wasn't unreasonable.

Besides, he'd always been a savvy negotiator. People loved to
bargain, they loved to dicker, they loved to land on a good price
together. He'd go up a few hundred thousand, and the seller would
come down a few hundred thousand, and everyone would shake hands
and leave the room happy.

Andrea nodded, tapped a note into her cell phone, and gave him a
smile. Real estate agent smiles, he observed, were a lot like Hollywood

smiles: automatic, bright, and not quite genuine. "Anything else?" she asked.

"Contingent on an inspection," he said.

"Of course."

"Okay, then." He slipped his sunglasses on, pulled his baseball cap more firmly onto his head, and gestured for Andrea to reenter the house ahead of him. He'd been raised in small-town Nebraska. He knew his manners.

Once they were inside, she locked the French doors. He followed her through the empty house, her high-heel shoes clicking and his sneakers squeaking against the hardwood floor. At the entry foyer, he paused. "You're not going to reveal my identity to the seller, right?" he asked.

"Your secret is safe with me," she promised. The smile she gave him when she said that seemed authentic.

He smiled back. "Just...you know." He shrugged. "People hear you're an actor and they get ideas." *Like the idea that you're richer than sin and can afford any price. Like the idea that you're going to turn the property into a pleasure palace, with naked swimming parties and candy dishes filled with cocaine instead of M&M's. Like the idea that you'll have starlets flocking to your house and fighting for access to your bed, and guests helicoptering into your back yard, and paparazzi chasing you down the street on motor scooters.*

Dylan was rich, but he didn't do drugs. He'd known a few starlets and he'd swum naked on occasion—although he'd done that a lot more often as a kid in Nebraska than as a movie star. He wanted to live in Brogan's Point because of the peace, the tranquility, the coziness—because it was everything Hollywood wasn't.

He and Andrea exited through the front door, a thick slab of oak with a diamond-shaped window of beveled glass embedded in it. Andrea checked to make sure it was locked, and then strolled with him down the brick front walk to where she'd parked her car. A brisk breeze rose off the ocean, scooping dead leaves from the ground and making them dance in the air. Living in Southern California, Dylan had missed the changing seasons. Here on the Massachusetts coast, some thirty miles north of Boston, he'd get his fill of blustery autumns and frigid winters.

Maybe in time he'd get sick of snow and ice. He doubted it, though.

He and Andrea didn't talk much during the drive back to the Ocean Bluff Inn, where he was staying. He'd had no trouble booking an ocean-view room there. Late autumn wasn't just a slow season for real estate sales; it was also a slow season for Brogan's Point in general. The locals he'd met six years ago had insisted that the town was always packed with visitors through the summer months and into mid-October, but once the fall foliage faded, so did the crowds.

That was fine. Crowds did nothing for him. If he lived in Brogan's Point, the cold, crowd-free days of winter would undoubtedly become his favorite time of year.

At the inn, he climbed out of Andrea's sedan, thanked her, and checked the time on his cell phone. Too early to eat dinner, let alone retire to his room for the evening. Restless, he watched her steer over the crushed shells and gravel of the parking area and down the winding drive to Atlantic Avenue. Once her car had disappeared down the road, he set off for that funky little bar he remembered from his visit to Brogan's Point six years ago.

He'd thought about going there last night, after he'd arrived at the inn. But he'd been jet-lagged, and he'd wound up drinking a scotch in his room while browsing the local real estate listings on his laptop. Better rested today, he'd visited four properties with Andrea. Three of them didn't have ocean views. The last one...yeah. Even if the owners refused to come down in price, Dylan could make it work.

He wished he could remember the name of the bar—the Something Street Pub? Six years ago, he and the crew had all been staying at a cheap motel on Route One; the charming Ocean Bluff

Inn had been way out of their price range. The eatery adjacent to that seedy motel had smelled of cooking grease and been too glaringly lit, so they'd located a bar in town for their after-work carousing. Not that they'd caroused much. They'd all been broke, laboring on a low-budget indie financed by overextended credit cards and the generosity of relatives.

The Something Street Pub had suited them perfectly. A little bit grungy, a little bit scruffy, decent prices and a friendly vibe. Dylan still remembered the antiquated jukebox standing against one wall, spitting out tunes three for a quarter. Where could anyone buy three of *anything* for a quarter?

He hoped the place still existed. Hanging out there had been one of the best things about working on location in Brogan's Point.

He might not be able to recall the name of the place, but he did recall that it was half a block off Atlantic Avenue, the boulevard that ran north-south, paralleling the town's coastline. He turned up the collar of his jacket and jammed his hands into his pockets as he strolled south on Atlantic. If he moved here—*when* he moved here—he'd have to invest in some sweaters and gloves. And a thick, woolen muffler. If he hinted loudly enough, one of his sisters might knit him one for Christmas.

He neared a side street that looked vaguely familiar. Turning the corner onto Faulk Street, he spotted the place. The Faulk Street Tavern, according to the sign beside the door.

A sharp gust of wind blew over the sea wall and across Atlantic Avenue, whipping his back. Even Mother Nature wanted him to hurry down Faulk Street to the bar.

He stepped inside and grinned as the atmosphere of the barroom settled over him, warming him like a favorite blanket. He didn't need his sunglasses indoors—he'd scarcely needed them outdoors in the fading late-afternoon sunlight struggling through the clouds. Would people recognize him if he took the glasses off? If they recognized him, would they do the whole fan thing? He was looking as scruffy and grungy as the pub itself these days, with his bristle of beard and his long, unkempt hair. A far cry from his familiar image as Captain Steele of the Galaxy Force. He might pass for Captain Steele's dissolute second cousin, but he was probably safe.

And if someone did recognize him, well, so be it. He'd be gracious. He's sign a napkin and pose for a selfie. It was thanks to the folks who cheered their way through the Galaxy Force movies that he could even contemplate buying a big, expensive house overlooking the ocean.

He tucked the sunglasses into a pocket of his jacket, pulled off his cap, and shook his hair loose. Avoiding eye contact with any of the patrons—an interesting collection of laborers, office workers, professionals, and people old enough to be retired—he strode directly to the bar and planted himself on a stool. The bartender who glided over to him was nearly as tall as he was, with short, reddish hair and a slim figure. "What can I get you?" she asked.

He considered ordering something hard, then opted for a beer. "What do you have on draft?"

She listed his choices, and he picked one at random. Once she'd set a chilled mug of beer and a bowl of bar snacks in front of him, he swiveled on the stool and surveyed the room.

There was the jukebox he'd remembered, garish and gorgeous, with its domed top, burled wood veneer, and stained-glass peacocks decorating the front panel. There were the booths along one wall and the tables along the other, with a small, square dance floor occupying the center of the room. The tables were filled people talking, arguing, laughing, drinking, snacking. No one was looking at him. He let out a long breath and took a sip. The beer was icy and sour. Perfect.

He'd resided in the Venice Beach neighborhood of Los Angeles for four years. Less than one day in Brogan's Point, and he felt more at home here than he'd ever felt there. Living in L.A. had been important at one time; when his career was just starting, he'd had to go to meetings, break bread with executives, schmooze the people in power. Even after the first Galaxy Force film turned out to be an unexpected blockbuster, launching a series and turning Dylan into a star as Captain Steele, he'd felt it important that he remain close to the film industry's beating heart.

Not anymore. His manager and his reps were in L.A. He could hop on a plane and be in Southern California in six hours if he was needed. And if he *wasn't* needed—if the producers and the director of *The Angel* decided, after three auditions, that they wanted to go with another actor—he could live wherever the hell he wanted, until someone was willing to cut him another big check to star in another film. Then...hop on a plane. He'd be there.

He watched as a dude in jeans and a dark blue work shirt with a company logo stitched above the breast pocket rose from a table, accompanied by hooting and guffaws from his companions, and shuffled over to the jukebox. He hunched over it for a long minute. The door to the tavern opened and a few more people swarmed in. Dylan pulled out his cell phone, skimmed a text from his manager that didn't say anything important, and checked the time. A few minutes past five. It was the TGIF celebration hour, the end of the work week. He predicted that the place would be packed before long.

The guy at the jukebox slid a coin into the slot, shrugged, and shuffled back to his friends at the table. The door swung open again, just as a song booted up, some ancient rock tune about a gypsy with a gold tooth—

That woman. He knew her.

She entered the bar with a man Dylan was sure he'd never seen before. But her... *Damn.* He recognized her at once—the tawny hair streaked with golden highlights, the delicately chiseled chin, the elegant cheekbones. The smile, when she spotted an empty booth, snagged the man's hand and pulled him across the dance floor to claim the table. The slender, graceful body half-hidden inside a heavy jacket, which she unzipped and shed before she slid onto the bench seat.

The smile. He knew that smile.

Six years ago. They'd both been a little drunk, a little giddy, but…

Damn. What was her name?

She settled into the booth, her back to the bar and Dylan. Just as well. If she recognized him, it could get awkward. Not that anything bad had happened between them so long ago. They'd met here at the bar, when the cast and crew had been celebrating their last day of location filming. His people had been mixing and mingling with the locals, buying rounds, having a grand old time. She'd flirted with him. He'd welcomed her advances. They'd both been looking for nothing more than a fun night—and hell, it had been fun. More than fun. It had been incredible. The best one-night-stand of his life.

But still… He couldn't even remember her freaking name. And she was with another guy now. It was pretty clear from their body language that they were a couple. Maybe married. Who knew? Six years was a long time.

He scrutinized the route between his stool and the exit. No way could he reach the door without crossing her line of vision. Of all the people in the bar, she'd be the one most likely to recognize him. The night they'd spent together, he hadn't yet become famous as Captain Steele. He'd just been Dylan Scott, a struggling actor in a low-budget indie, with messy hair and a stubble of beard, just like he had now.

Then again, she might have forgotten all about him and that night. He hadn't thought about her for the past six years. She might not have thought about him, either. There she was, chatting with the waitress taking her order while her companion looked on. He appeared older than her, his hair starting to thin, his jaw as square as a box of crackers.

Gwen. Her name came to Dylan in a sudden pop of memory. *Gwen.*

God, they'd been good together that night. Better than good. Phenomenal.

A lifetime ago.

He needed to leave. Now. Before she spotted him.

He drained his mug of beer, tossed a twenty onto the bar, and eased off the stool. He decided not to hide behind his sunglasses. In the bar's dim lighting, wearing them would call more attention to him than leaving them off. If he cut a path past the tables, across the dance floor from the booths, he might be able to sneak out without her noticing.

His escape would be easier if some of the patrons did him the favor of dancing. What was wrong with them? The voice from the jukebox was wailing about a love potion. They should be on their feet, crowding the floor, obscuring her view of Dylan while he made his getaway.

But no. Everyone remained seated, drinking and chattering, providing no cover.

The waitress left Gwen's table, and Gwen steered her attention back to her companion. Now, while she was caught up in a conversation, was Dylan's best chance to walk across the room unnoticed. He moved toward the wall on the table side of the room, his head forward and his steps decisive. He could do this. She'd never see him.

When he was ten feet from the door, the love potion song ended and the jukebox began playing another song. Some gentle guitar notes, a muted horn, and then a woman's voice, sweet and crystal-clear.

He'd never heard this song before, either, but it froze him in place. The woman sang about no strings, no love, no commitment. Simply goodbye. Goodbye after a night together. "Just call me angel of the morning," she sang, her voice fierce yet aching, sorrowful yet determined.

Something in the song compelled Dylan to glance toward the table where Gwen sat. She was staring at him, her pale eyes wide, her lips parted in surprise.

Shit. She'd seen him, and she'd recognized him. *Of all the gin joints in all the world*—the famous line from *Casablanca* spun through his head. Except that *he* was the one who'd entered *her* gin joint. Brogan's Point was her world, not his.

Not yet, anyway.

He tried to move closer to the door, but the song exerted some sort of spell on him, paralyzing him where he stood. The singer urged him to turn away, promised she would not beg him to stay—but he couldn't move. He could only stand there, listening to her beg to be called angel of the morning.

What did that even mean? Why couldn't he get the hell out of here?

Why wouldn't Gwen look away? Was she paralyzed, too?

Minutes passed. "Just touch my cheek before you leave," the morning angel sang. If Dylan touched Gwen's cheek, would he be able to leave?

He couldn't touch her. Couldn't march over to her table and say, "Hi, remember me? Remember that spectacular night, when I had you screaming and you had me groaning, and in the morning we just…" *Left.* Touched each other, and left.

The song faded out to silence, and Dylan bolted for the door

Chapter Two

Gwen felt as if she was waking up from a dream.

Not a dream. A nightmare.

What on earth was Dylan Scott doing in Brogan's Point? Why wasn't he thousands of miles away in Hollywood, living his glamorous life and forgetting she'd ever existed?

"Gwen?" Mike snapped his fingers just inches from her nose, startling her. "I said, should we order a pizza here, or should we stop at Dominic's?"

As if she gave a damn where they got pizza. She didn't want pizza. She didn't even like pizza that much. Mike started babbling about how the pizza they served at the Faulk Street Tavern was more of a flat-bread type with a crunchy crust, the sauce better than it had been a year ago...and all she could think of was that song, and Dylan Scott standing across the room, staring at her.

Bad enough that he was in town. Worse, he'd seen her—and apparently recognized her, if his flagrant staring was anything to go by.

"I don't feel well," she said, gazing at her hands so she wouldn't have to look directly at Mike. "I'd like to go home."

"Don't be ridiculous," he argued. "We've already ordered our drinks." The look she flashed at him must have expressed her annoyance, because he added, in a gentler tone, "You got a sitter. It would be a crime to let a good sitter go to waste."

True enough. Lining up a babysitter on a Friday night was never easy, but Gwen had managed to find one. Kerry was only twelve, but it wasn't as if she had to change diapers or warm a bottle. Gwen had left tuna salad, rolls, pickles, some sliced prosciutto, and a tub of chocolate ice-cream for Kerry and Annie to feast on, and two Pixar videos to watch. She needed to take advantage of her free evening. Mike was surely expecting them to return to his apartment for sex before he brought her home.

11

That had been her expectation, too, before she'd spotted Dylan Scott standing near the bar's exit, staring at her while the song from the jukebox wafted around them. When she'd hired Kerry, she'd figured she and Mike would indulge in a little naked horizontal time before they called it a night. She enjoyed making love with Mike. He wasn't the most exciting lover she'd ever had, but excitement was no longer a top priority for her.

Not that she'd had all that many exciting lovers in her life. A couple of guys in college, including Adam, the love of her life, whom she'd been sure she would marry—until she realized that no, they wouldn't marry, after all. And Mike.

And, for one crazy night, after Adam but long before Mike, Dylan Scott.

He shouldn't count, certainly not as a lover. *Love* had had nothing to do with that night. It had been just a crazy fling, a mindless bit of fun that had ended with the sunrise. If not for Annie, she would never have given him another thought.

But there *was* Annie. And now there was this: Dylan Scott was back in town. Dylan was back, and that song...

"Did you hear that song?" she asked Mike.

He frowned, gaping at her as if she were insane—which she very well might be. "'Let's Spend the Night Together,'" he named it. "Famous for being censored on some TV show. The Stones had to sing 'Let's spend some time together'—"

"No. The song before that one."

Mike frowned again, struggling to recall the previous song. "Some chick tune. Never heard it before."

Gwen had never heard it before, either. But it echoed inside her, soulful and stoical. *I won't beg you to stay,* the woman had sung. *Call me angel of the morning.*

The waitress appeared with their drinks, and Mike ordered a flatbread pepperoni pizza. Gwen leaned back in her seat, resigned to the fact that they would not be leaving the Faulk Street Tavern anytime soon. They would eat their pizza, and Mike would analyze the sauce, and he'd tell her about his lineup at Wright Honda-BMW tomorrow, where he was a salesman and Saturdays were his busiest day of the week. She'd nod and smile when necessary, and she'd choke down some of the pizza, and after they were done eating, she'd try to pretend the sex was okay. She'd ask Mike to take her home as soon as they were done. She'd pay Kerry, and Mike would drive her back to her house down the street from Gwen's, and Gwen would straighten up the kitchen and put the DVD's away. She'd kiss her slumbering daughter and climb into bed, and pray with all her heart that by the time she woke up tomorrow morning, Dylan Scott would be gone.

***

Gus Naukonen lifted the empty beer mug, her gaze on the tavern door as it swung shut behind the actor from the Galaxy Force movies. She'd recognized him right away, despite his slacker grooming. He'd been at the Faulk Street Tavern before, years ago, when that art film about a struggling family of fishermen was being made on location in Brogan's Point.

Something in the song from the jukebox had clearly spooked him.

Gus possessed a great memory when it came to patrons—even patrons who hadn't been inside her establishment in years—and a pretty good memory when it came to the songs the jukebox played. She couldn't recall ever hearing it play that particular song before. It was a pretty ballad, the woman's voice thick with emotion, with irony. You could tell the singer cared very much about the lover who was leaving her, even as she sang that his leaving meant nothing to her. It sure as hell meant something.

The door opened again, and a few new customers entered. Not Ed Nolan. He'd stopped by earlier for his afternoon cup of coffee, and he'd probably stop by again after his shift ended. When you were a police detective on a small-town force, shifts didn't end precisely at five. They ended when a case was closed, an arrest made, a ream of paperwork processed. He'd get here when he got here, and she'd have another cup of coffee waiting for him, or maybe a beer. He allowed himself an occasional drink now and then.

He wanted to marry her, but she saw no reason to complicate their relationship by getting married. With his daughter and her two sons to consider, they'd probably have to write pre-nups, or separate their estates, or whatever. Why bother? He wasn't going to touch her cheek and walk away, as the guy did according to the lyrics of that poignant song. Gus wasn't going to walk away from Ed, either.

She set the dirty glass on the dishwasher rack for Manny to deal with, then gazed at the door again. The jukebox was playing a Rolling Stones song, and it didn't seem to be affecting anyone. Gus wasn't sure, though. That sweet young woman who owned the Attic—Gwen Parker—looked anxious, even anguished. Maybe because her boyfriend was kind of a jerk. A nice jerk, but not good enough for her, in Gus's opinion.

No, Gwen's uneasiness had begun before Mick Jagger's nasal wail filled the room. She'd reacted to the previous song. *Angel of the Morning.*

Gwen and the movie actor? Why would the song have cast a spell on the two of them? They had nothing in common, no point of intersection. A local shop owner and Captain Steele of the Galaxy Force?

Maybe the jukebox had made a mistake.

Gus doubted it, though. The jukebox never made a mistake. That was part of its magic.

Chapter Three

The breakfast menu in the main restaurant at the Ocean Bluff Inn did nothing for Dylan. No doubt all those fluffy farm omelets and wild berry pancakes would taste delicious. But he'd slept poorly and awakened unsettled. The prospect of swallowing anything more substantial than a cup of coffee didn't appeal to him.

He tried to revive himself with a shower, but while the steamy water sharpened his brain, it did nothing for his appetite. He felt drowsy and restless at the same time, yearning to crawl back into bed yet eager to head out into town and accomplish something, although he had no idea what.

He checked his phone. No messages from Andrea Simonetti. A note from his manager saying nothing. He stuffed the phone into a pocket of his jacket, then left the room. Descending to the first floor, he waved at the friendly lady behind the registration counter. She waved back, and he stepped outside into the chilly New England morning.

The veranda spanning the front of the inn was longer than the back porch on the house he hoped to buy, and it held several Adirondack chairs and a few potted plants that were clinging desperately to their last few days of life, before frost finished them off. He allowed himself a moment to imagine how he'd furnish the porch on the house he hoped to buy—maybe a rocker, maybe lounge chair wide enough for two, in case a helicopter landed in his back yard and a beautiful naked starlet climbed out.

With a chuckle, he descended the steps to the parking lot and unlocked his rental car. It was a staid Toyota Camry, a far cry from his hot little Porsche back in California. He wondered how the Porsche would handle during New England's harsh winters. He'd probably have to buy a big, bulky four-wheel-drive vehicle to get around in the snow.

But first he had to buy the house. And so far, Andrea hadn't reported on how the current owners had reacted to his opening bid.

The Toyota drove well and didn't call attention to itself, so he was satisfied with it. He cruised down the inn's driveway to Atlantic Avenue and south, not sure where he was going until he reached a quiet block of shops and boutiques. One had a sign above the door featuring two huge cookies that created the two O's in the word "Cookie's." Would a store called "Cookie's" sell coffee? He might not be hungry, but he could use some caffeine.

He parked, climbed out of the car, and entered the store. The aroma of baked goods jolted his appetite, as did the stack of date-nut bars on display in the glass-enclosed case below the counter. The woman behind the counter plucked a couple of cookies from a shelf and handed them to a wiry couple in jogging gear and wool caps. They paid, then strode out of the eatery, their oversized cookies destined to undermine whatever they'd accomplished with their morning run.

Dylan stepped up to the counter. "I'll have one of those date bars and a large coffee," he said.

The woman regarded him for a long minute. "You look like Captain Steele. Hey—you *are* Captain Steele, aren't you?"

He'd been prepared to pay with cash rather than a credit card in order to protect his identity, but it was too late to remain incognito. The woman was already shouting over her shoulder: "Hey, Maeve, get out here! It's Captain Steele!"

He exerted himself to be pleasant. If he did wind up living in Brogan's Point, people around town would eventually get used to him. He'd just be Dylan, the guy who lived in that sprawling old Victorian overlooking the ocean on the north end of town. The guy who roared around town in a bright yellow Porsche Carrera and vanished for a months at a time when he was filming on location, and visited sick kids in hospitals every chance he got—usually clad in his Captain Steele costume—and occasionally appeared in some gossip column with a gorgeous actress hanging off his arm.

All right, so he wouldn't exactly blend in. But maybe in time, people would think of him as someone other than Captain Steele.

Right now, Captain Steele was exactly how the clerk was thinking of him. She was promptly joined by a younger, prettier woman in a white apron. They babbled about the Galaxy Force movies, and the older woman recalled when Dylan had come to town years ago to film that low-budget indie, an event that occurred at a time the younger woman wasn't living in Brogan's Point. "I would have made a fool of myself if Captain Steele had been in my little town," the younger woman said. "I love those movies. They're like popcorn!"

"Junk food," Dylan joked.

"Healthy junk food." She grinned. "But not as healthy as my date nut bars."

He didn't point out that Captain Steele was in her little town now and she wasn't really making a fool of herself. Nor did he mention that when he'd last been in Brogan's Point, the first Galaxy Force movie was still more than a month from its release date, and at the time, no one had known what a blockbuster it would turn out to be. He'd been a hard-working unknown actor then, like all the other actors in *Sea Glass*, trying to create something artistic and worthwhile.

No point in going into all that. He politely posed for a selfie with the two women and then departed.

Outside, he strolled down the street, munching on the bar—which tasted so good, he decided he must have been hungry, after all. By the time he'd reached the corner, he'd devoured the entire thing—and he knew why he had driven to this block. There, just across the street, was the Attic.

Six years ago, when he'd last been in Brogan's Point, pretty much everyone involved in *Sea Glass* had visited the Attic at least once. Its merchandise was eclectic—knickknacks, art objects, vintage apparel, accessories, stuff that looked antique but wasn't. There were snow globes, real globes, chess sets with pieces that resembled the British

Redcoats and the Colonists during the Revolutionary War. There were boxes of notecards featuring paintings of the ocean. There were long, narrow implements the shop's owner had identified as clam shovels, for digging clams out of the sand. There were hair ornaments and tooled belts, candles and kerosene lamps, coffee mugs and collectable teaspoons, a complete mishmash of merchandise, all of which seemed to define the culture of a seaside New England town.

"It's called the Attic," the pretty young saleswoman had explained when he'd come to the store with the director and the production designer in search of items to dress the film's set and accessorize the actors, "because it's filled with the kinds of things you'd find in someone's attic. If you don't find what you like today, come back tomorrow. Our inventory changes every day."

The saleswoman had been Gwen.

He wondered if she still worked there. He wondered why he'd driven to this street, to the store where he'd first met her. Some strange instinct? Some compulsion to see her again?

He reminded himself that what had happened six years ago had been a blink of time, and that when he'd seen Gwen last night, she'd been with a man. She was probably married.

Still, saying hello to her shouldn't cause any problems. Besides, he might find something he wanted to buy in the store. If the displays in its front windows were anything to go by, it still offered an intriguing variety of items for sale. Once he owned a house here in town, he'd get one of those Revolutionary War chess sets for the den.

He surveyed the displays in the windows while he sipped his coffee. When his cup was empty, he entered the store.

It looked larger than he remembered. It *was* larger, having expanded to occupy the adjacent store. Business must be good.

A few other customers roamed around the store. Shelves and tables stood at interesting angles, forcing shoppers to meander rather than simply march up one aisle and down another. A nook in the back corner was filled with children's books. A sloping rack displayed an assortment of dresses that might have been in style during the Roaring Twenties. A shelf along one wall held decorative boxes, their lids inlaid with stained-wood mosaics, depicting images of the sea. An umbrella stand was filled with wooden walking sticks, their handles carved into animal faces: a hawk, a panther, a spaniel with floppy ears.

The attic in the Dylan's childhood home had contained some boxes filled with tax records, some clear plastic cases containing old blankets that smelled of camphor, and cartons of discarded pots and pans that his mother had saved for when Dylan and his two sisters set up their own homes. By the time Dylan and his sisters were adults, moving out into the world, they'd preferred to buy their own pots and pans. For all he knew, those cartons of cookware were still collecting dust in his parents' attic.

If the house he'd grown up in had had an attic like this store, he probably would have never gone outside to play. He would have spent all his free hours upstairs under the eaves, exploring.

A clerk wandered over to him. "Can I help you find something?" she asked.

"No, I'm just browsing," he said, then hesitated. "Does Gwen still work here?"

"Gwen? Sure, she's in the back. I'll go get her."

Dylan wasn't sure he was ready to see Gwen yet. No one had given him a script to memorize, so he didn't know what he would say once they were face to face. But the clerk was being much too helpful, bounding through the store before he could stop her and vanishing through a door near the children's books.

He ran a hand through his hair, wondering whether he should have worn his baseball cap. Or his sunglasses. Not that he could conceal his identity from Gwen. After they'd shared that song in the bar yesterday—if you could call staring at each other across a crowded room sharing—she'd recognize him.

He distracted himself by studying a collection of scrimshaw pieces displayed on a shelf to his right. Each piece was unique—delicate seascapes painted in thin black lines on polished bone. His parents might like one of these. Scrimshaw wasn't exactly ubiquitous in Nebraska. They'd be the only folks in town to own a painted whalebone.

He lifted one of the pieces and studied it more closely. The whaling ship depicted on the smooth white surface could have belonged to Ahab. Dylan had read *Moby-Dick* in college and hadn't liked it much, but he'd loved the idea of living on the ocean. He still loved the idea.

"Dylan."

He hadn't heard her approach, but her voice reached him, velvet-soft. He didn't remember her voice being so muted. She'd been pretty loud in bed. When she'd come...

Don't think about that. He placed the scrimshaw piece back on the shelf and turned.

Gwen's voice might not match his memory, but her face did. She was still pretty in a fresh, unadorned way, her features delicate, her eyes a sweet pussy-willow gray fringed with thick lashes a shade darker than her hair. She wore a burgundy sweater and beige slacks, and her hair hung tousled past her shoulders. *Bed head,* he thought as his body clenched with another memory of her in bed beside him, beneath him, taking him in.

He sucked in a sharp breath, then smiled. He was an actor; he could do this. "Hi, Gwen."

"What are you doing here?"

"Shopping?"

She struggled to return his smile. "I mean in Brogan's Point. Aren't you supposed to be in Hollywood?"

He shrugged. "I have a few months free before we begin shooting the next Galaxy Force movie. I thought I'd..." He hesitated before saying he'd thought he'd buy a house in Brogan's Point. Gwen seemed less than thrilled to have him standing in her store. That he was planning to buy a house in her town might send her screaming—and not in ecstasy. "Looks like the store is doing well," he said instead. "It's about double the size I remember."

"It's doing fine," she said tersely.

Screw this. They'd gotten along beautifully the last time he'd seen her. Why was she treating him as if he were contagious? "Look. I didn't come here to cause you problems, okay? I came because...you know. We had a good time together six years ago. That's all."

Her cheeks flushed a delicate pink. Evidently she remembered just how good a time they'd had together. She turned her attention to the scrimshaw, shifting the piece he'd been admiring as if he'd put it back in the wrong place. "I'm sorry. It's just—" She fidgeted with Ahab's whaling ship a bit more, then lifted her face to meet his gaze. "That song. Yesterday, at the Faulk Street Tavern..."

So he hadn't imagined that the song had affected her as strangely as it had affected him. "Yeah. That was pretty weird, wasn't it."

"Supposedly, that jukebox is magic."

He laughed. She allowed herself a faint smile, but apparently she wasn't joking. "Magic?"

"Just an old wives' tale." She pulled her hand back from the shelf. She seemed to be struggling to add some warmth to her smile, but she wasn't doing a good job of it. Her eyes were glassy, focused not quite on his face but on something behind him, something only she could see. "Well. I've got to get back to work. It was nice of you to drop by. I hope you enjoy your visit."

He was about to tell her—to warn her, really—that this wasn't just a visit, that he was hoping to move to town. But before he could speak, a child's voice rang through the store, happily shrill: "Mommy! Look at the picture I drawed!"

The color drained from Gwen's complexion. She spun away from Dylan and squatted down in time to greet a fireball of a girl racing

---

through the maze of aisles, chased by another girl who appeared to be in her late teens. The child wore jeans, a bright pink sweatshirt with sparkly stars on it, and sneakers with more sparkly stars glittering across the toes. Her hair was a mess of chestnut curls, her eyes big and dark, her cheeks adorably round and punctuated by deep dimples. She clutched a sheet of paper in her hand.

"Look, Mommy! It's Mr. Snuffy!" she shouted, shoving the paper at Gwen.

Gwen took the paper and studied it intently. Dylan studied the girl just as intently. She looked a lot like Marissa, his nine-year-old niece.

In fact, she looked almost exactly like Marissa when Marissa had been in kindergarten.

Five years old? Was that the age of this little girl who was calling Gwen Mommy?

"I'm sorry," the teenage girl said, then giggled. "I tried to stop her, but she was so excited—"

"That's a wonderful drawing," Gwen said, her affectionate tone a sharp contrast to the ice in her voice when she'd spoken to Dylan. "It looks a lot like Mr. Snuffy." Dylan glanced at the drawing and concluded that Mr. Snuffy, whoever he was, was exceedingly brown and misshapen, with a fat tail and uneven ears. A dog, maybe, or a fox. Possibly an obese squirrel. "But I'm with a customer right now, sweetie, so you'll have to go back to the office. I'll be in in a minute, okay?" Gwen ruffled her fingers through the little girl's curls, kissed her brow, and then stood back up. She remained with her back to Dylan, watching the older girl escort the child back through the store and away.

Dylan watched them, too. He watched that little girl with her dancing curls and her dark eyes, eyes nothing like her mother's.

Eyes like his niece's.

Eyes like his.

Holy shit.

Before Gwen could turn back to him, he was out of the store, his heart racing, his fingers numb, his scalp tightening around his skull as if it wanted to squeeze the possibilities out of his brain. But there were only two possibilities he could think of. Either Gwen had adopted that little girl at some point after Dylan had left Brogan's Point and moved on with his life, or...

Holy shit.

Chapter Four

He was gone.

Gwen supposed she should have expected as much. She'd tried to tell him way back at the beginning, and he'd blown her off. If he'd cared, if he'd had half an ounce of responsibility in his gorgeous body, he could have responded, taken steps, behaved decently. But he hadn't done a damned thing—except to ignore her.

That was then. This was now. He'd been confronted with the truth. He might make a different choice today than he had six years ago. That possibility scared the hell out of Gwen.

He'd seen Annie. He'd figured things out. Maybe the sight of her jarred his memory of the emails Gwen had sent back then, pleading with him to get in touch with her. He was six years older and more mature. Maybe he would think he ought to honor the obligation he'd so blithely dismissed when it might have made a difference.

If he wanted to pay child support, Gwen wasn't too proud to take it. The extra money could mean a lot to Annie.

But if Dylan Scott wanted to become a part of Annie's life, to be her *father*...

Forget it. That ship had sailed.

Gwen moved the piece of scrimshaw Dylan had been examining a fraction of an inch to the left, as if by repositioning it she could nullify his having touched it. Her gaze drifted to the store's entry. He sure had bolted fast. Not the behavior of someone who wanted to bond with his long-lost daughter.

A vague queasiness overtook Gwen, and she turned away from the door. Who knew what he'd do? He had millions of dollars. He was Captain Steele, after all. He could hire lawyers. He could demand custody. He could take Gwen's daughter from her, and change her name from Annie Parker to Annie Scott.

No, he couldn't. He might have money, but Gwen had Annie. She had five amazing, challenging, love-filled years as her daughter's loving mommy. No court could take Annie away from her.

Even so, she probably ought to hire a lawyer. Just in case.

More queasiness. She was getting along okay, the store profitable, the monthly mortgage payments on her house covered without too much hardship, Annie well dressed and adequately supplied with crayons, books, and stuffed animals. But hiring a lawyer was expensive. Gwen wasn't sure she had enough of a financial cushion for that. Especially if she would be battling a Hollywood star.

Then again, what could a Hollywood star possibly want with a demanding five-year-old daughter? Dylan was probably halfway back to California already, running for his life. Gwen would never see him again. They were nothing to each other, nothing other than victims of one long-ago night.

Where had that notion come from? She'd never thought of herself as a victim before. Yet the phrase resonated inside her head: *Victims of the night.*

She realized it was a line from that song, the plaintive ballad the jukebox had played yesterday when she'd spotted Dylan at the Faulk Street Tavern. Weird that she'd never heard the song before, yet some of its lyrics had imprinted themselves on her memory. *Victims of the night.* Gwen wondered what the phrase referred to, what it meant.

Giving her head a resolute shake, she hurried through the store to the staff rooms in the back. The hallway at the rear of the building led to several storage rooms that held her inventory, an employee restroom, a snack room barely large enough to contain a mini-fridge, a microwave, and a coffee maker, and her office. She'd devoted a significant chunk of that office to Annie.

Running a store as a single mother was tougher than anything Gwen had ever done before. Some mothers worked weekdays from nine to five and were able to spend their entire weekends with their children. For Gwen, though, Saturday was the Attic's busiest day of the week. She had an excellent assistant manager who oversaw things from noon until closing time on Saturday and all day Sunday, but Gwen felt she owed it to her staff and her customers to spend Saturday mornings at the store. Fortunately, she'd found the perfect employee in Jenny, who didn't mind babysitting Annie in the morning as long as Gwen let her work the cash register in the afternoon. She was a sophomore in high school, barely old enough to work legally. But she loved the store, and she'd started pestering Gwen for a job even before her sixteenth birthday. As soon as Gwen could hire Jenny without breaking the law, she had—as a part-time babysitter and a part-time cashier.

Gwen found them in her office, where they usually spent their Saturday mornings. Annie sat at a tyke-size school desk Gwen had rescued from one of the estate-liquidation hauls her friend Diana Simms had brought her a few months ago. The surface of the desk was covered with paper and crayons. Mr. Snuffy, Annie's bedraggled stuffed dog, was propped up on another chair. He was the ideal artist's model, sitting perfectly motionless while Annie captured him with her box of sixty-four colors. The drawing Annie had raced into the store to show Gwen was one of about eight; across the desk top lay several lesser efforts. Gwen hoped Mr. Snuffy appreciated being the subject of so many portraits.

"You know who that guy looked like?" Jenny said as she picked a couple of crayons up off the floor.

Gwen nodded. "Yes. He's the actor who stars in those silly space movies."

"Really? That was him? Are you sure?"

Gwen nodded.

"Oh, my God! I would have taken his picture. I don't know—maybe he wouldn't have let me. He's so cute!"

More charismatic than cute, Gwen would have argued, but she let the comment pass.

"The Galaxy Force movies aren't silly," Jenny said. "They're allegories." She must have been paying attention in her English class.

Gwen allowed that the movies weren't that silly. But the only movie of Dylan's that had truly touched her had been *Sea Glass*, the film that had brought him to Brogan's Point. *Sea Glass* hadn't survived long in the theaters. It was too quiet—a family drama without a single car chase or explosion in it. A month after the cast and crew had decamped, the first Galaxy Force film had been released, and it had been such a huge success, *Sea Glass* went all but forgotten.

Gwen hadn't forgotten it, however. She'd bought her own copy as soon as it had been released on DVD, and she'd viewed it more times than she'd care to admit. She'd sat in her darkened living room, long after tucking Annie into bed, and watched the sweet, moving story of a modest family in a seaside town, struggling in the aftermath of the patriarch's death. He'd been a fisherman, and he'd drowned at sea. Dylan had played his son, determined to take his father's place at the helm of his fishing boat, the Sea Glass. His mother wanted any other future for him but that. The ocean had claimed her husband, and she couldn't bear the possibility that it might claim her son, as well.

It was a beautiful film. A small film, as the critics liked to call arty, subtle movies like *Sea Glass*, filmed on a shoestring budget with a bunch of then-unknown actors. No one had predicted that the space opera Dylan had filmed just before joining the cast of *Sea Glass* would be so enormously successful, launching a blockbuster franchise. No one had foreseen that the handsome, sensitive actor who'd played Tommy in *Sea Glass* would suddenly become famous as Captain Steele.

If that movie's an allegory, Gwen thought with a sniff, *it's an allegory about gaining fame while losing your humanity.*

Had fame and fortune changed Dylan Scott? She had no idea. She hadn't really known him then, and she knew him even less now.

She'd be a fool to believe he hadn't changed, of course. Look at how much *she'd* changed. Back then, she'd been...well, the sort of woman who'd spend a night in bed with a near stranger. No promises, no professions of love. *No strings to bind your hands.*

She caught her breath. Another line from the song she'd heard yesterday at the Faulk Street Tavern. How had it taken root in her mind? Why?

"Can we have lunch at Riley's?" Annie asked, gazing up hopefully at her mother.

Gwen was startled by how much Annie resembled Dylan. She had never really thought about it before. Possibly that was because in his incarnation as Captain Steele he was clean-cut and polished, and Annie never looked clean-cut or polished, even after she climbed out of the bath. Mostly, however, it was because Gwen thought about Dylan as rarely as possible. True, he was her daughter's father, and his name appeared on Annie's birth certificate. At some point—in the distant future, Gwen had always assumed—she would tell Annie about him.

But not now. Not when she and Mike were finally figuring things out, and he was easing gradually into the role of Annie's step-father. He'd already proposed to Gwen, well aware that marrying her meant accepting Annie, too. Gwen hadn't said yes to him, but she planned to, once she felt Annie was ready to share her mother with Mike.

The last thing Gwen needed was Dylan Scott barging in and screwing everything up.

"I think we'll go home for lunch," she told Annie. What she really thought was, if she was going to have to hire a lawyer, she'd better start counting her pennies. Riley's offered big portions at small prices, but still, Gwen could feed Annie for less at home. "I've got peanut butter and bananas. You know what that means, right?"

"Ice-cream!" Annie said, then broke into laughter. "For *dessert*, Mommy."

Gwen laughed, too. The hell with Dylan. He'd had his chance to laugh with his daughter, and he'd blown it.

***

The Faulk Street Tavern was packed that night. Everyone in town had loved having the film folks around, adding a little glamor and stardust to their sleepy seaside town, and everyone wanted to party with them. The Hollywood people weren't really "Hollywood" people. They'd always behaved down-to-earth and modest, making few demands and apologizing when they had to block off a street or a wharf for filming, even though they'd gotten permissions and licenses from Town Hall. Really, they were very nice.

Besides, they'd spent lots of money in town. During the summer, Brogan Point bustled with beach people, but things tended to quiet down in the autumn, especially after the foliage had peaked and the leaf-peepers had departed. Except for December, when holiday shoppers packed the place, the Attic generally saw about half the amount of traffic in the off months as it did in the summer.

A woman named Linnette, who'd been introduced to Gwen as the movie's artistic designer, had wandered through the Attic several times, buying items she thought would give the actors' costumes and the scenery an authentic New England feel. Gwen didn't understand movie stuff, but she understood what Linnette was looking for and helped her to choose items that would add that authenticity. Like a film designer, Gwen was an expert at creating appealing atmospherics. A store had to look inviting. It had to be arranged in a way that made customers want to come in and browse—and buy. She imagined that adorning a film with the right candles or clocks or umbrellas was just as important as arranging a store's merchandise.

On a few of her shopping sprees, Linnette had brought other people from the film to the Attic with her. Gwen had met the director, a big, bearded bear of a guy in rumpled jeans and T-shirts with a variety of political slogans printed across them. Linnette had also introduced her to a couple of the cast members. When Dylan had accompanied Linnette on one visit, he and Gwen had had a fine time talking about the Midwest. He was from Nebraska and she'd grown up in central Illinois. They'd both appreciated the sight, the scent, the feel of the ocean in a way people who'd grown up near the coast never would. Unlike Brogan's Point natives, they didn't take the salty fragrance, the humid breezes, and the constant lullaby of waves breaking against the beach for granted.

So she'd headed to the Faulk Street Tavern on the crew's last night, when they were celebrating the wrap of their location filming. She'd broken up with Adam just a couple of weeks earlier, and she'd been feeling lonely and vulnerable. Partying with the film people seemed like a good distraction. She needed to learn how to have fun as a single woman, now that she was no longer one-half of a couple.

She couldn't pinpoint exactly when she and Dylan Scott, her fellow Midwesterner, found each other among the boisterous crowd. Pitchers of beer were being rapidly emptied. Music was blaring. People were dancing, singing along, chattering, hugging, posing for photos. She drank more than usual—not enough to get drunk, but enough to sand the sharp edge off her sorrow over her break-up with Adam. Enough to make her feel carefree, ready to have fun.

And Dylan was so handsome. Not pretty-boy handsome like some movie stars, but handsome in an accessible way, his cocoa-brown eyes warm and inviting, his prominent nose balanced by his prominent chin, his smile easy and natural. One of his front teeth was slightly crooked, she'd noticed. Didn't movie stars get their teeth straightened and bleached?

He wasn't really a movie star, though. He might be starring in Sea Glass, *but it wasn't as if he'd appeared on the covers of celebrity magazines or been a guest on late-night talk shows. He was just...Dylan.*

They talked. They drank beer. They danced—not dirty dancing, they barely touched—but when he did touch her, she felt special. Being touched by a man who wasn't Adam at first seemed weird, and then not weird at all. Dylan was fun. No emotions were involved, no commitments, nothing but the pleasure of two people cutting loose and having a good time, burning off stress and reveling in the physical pleasure of moving together, sharing a carefree pocket of time with each other.

At some point, they chose to leave. At some point, she drove with him to the motel on Route One where the film people had been staying. At some point, they entered his room and locked the door behind them.

He had the most beautiful body she'd ever seen. He was lean and wiry, not an ounce of excess flesh on him. His muscles were sleek and supple, not pumped up. His hands were graceful as he lifted her sweater over her head, as he eased her jeans down her legs. He kissed like an angel, sweet, soft kisses that lured rather than demanded, that gave more than they took.

For her first time with a man who wasn't Adam, she couldn't have chosen better. Dylan asked nothing of her, just that she enjoy the encounter as much as he did. And she did enjoy it. More than enjoy it. He'd made her come so many times that night, she wasn't sure she'd be able to walk in the morning.

They used protection. But she'd stopped taking the pill when she and Adam had ended things, wanting to give her body a break, and as she later learned, woman were often much more fertile in the first weeks after discontinuing oral contraceptives. And condoms were only about ninety percent effective, or something like that.

What did it matter? Dylan was long gone by the time Gwen discovered she was pregnant.

Long gone and unreachable.

Long gone and beyond caring.

Chapter Five

Dylan sat in his rental car, trying to center his thoughts. Through his window, the two big chocolate-chip cookies in the Cookie's sign stared at him like accusing eyes. *Don't blame me,* he wanted to shout at them. *I had no idea.*

What kind of bitch was Gwen, that she hadn't told him? Did she think he wouldn't want to know that he'd fathered a child?

His heart pounded, slamming against his ribs with each beat. His breath rasped in his throat. A *father.* How could he have become a father?

Well, he knew how. Nothing particularly complicated about that. If he was remembering correctly, they had used condoms. But there were all those statistics about failure rates, and he and Gwen had had a few drinks, and they'd been going at it with such feverish enthusiasm, he shouldn't be surprised that they'd slipped up. His mind hadn't been its sharpest that night. The expression "screwing one's brains out" seemed an appropriate description for the night he'd spent with Gwen. He had some pretty graphic memories of how they'd passed the hours, but *thinking*? No, they hadn't done much of that.

He pulled his cell phone out of his pocket and tapped in Andrea Simonetti's number. Real estate salespeople worked Saturdays, and she answered on the second ring. "Hi, Dylan. Nothing to report," she told him. "I relayed your offer to the seller's broker, but she hasn't gotten back to me yet."

"Okay," Dylan said, pretending that seeking an update on his bid was his reason for calling. "If they really want to sell, they'll come back with a counter-offer."

"I'm sure. These things take time, of course."

Blah-blah-blah. Small talk, shop talk. Impatient, his heart still thumping against his rib cage like a prisoner attempting a jail break,

Dylan steered the conversation in a different direction. "So, I was wondering—you know that store, the Attic?"

"Oh, I love that store," Andrea gushed. "Whenever I go in there, I find something new. The inventory constantly changes. It's like an adventure every time."

"Yeah." Dylan did his best to sound as if he shared Andrea's enthusiasm for the place. "Do you know the name of that pretty sales clerk?"

"Gwen Parker, you mean? She's the owner. She's worked like a dog to turn that place around. The previous owner—what was her name? Janice Something. Total flake. Good at conceptualizing, but the place always looked kind of drab and sad—like a real attic, I guess. But she retired and sold the business to Gwen. And Gwen lit a fire under the place. Not literally, of course." Andrea chuckled at her own joke. "I've gotten to know her through the Brogan's Point Business Association. She always has great ideas at our meetings. Ways to spruce up downtown at the holidays, ways to make parking easier. She's a real spitfire."

She'd been a spitfire that night six years ago, Dylan thought. But his brain locked onto *Gwen Parker*. Bless Andrea for having supplied him with Gwen's last name, and the news that she now owned the business.

He let the broker yammer for a minute more, then extricated himself from the call. As soon as it ended, he tapped his phone screen to open a browser, navigated to the White Pages, and typed "Gwen Parker Brogan's Point MA."

An address for Gwendolyn Parker appeared. *Gwendolyn.*

She went from being Gwen to being Gwendolyn Parker in his mind. She went from being a fantastic sex partner to a successful shop owner. And a mother.

And a spitfire.

And a selfish bitch who'd neglected to let him know he was a father.

He clicked over to GPS and tapped in her address. In less than ten minutes, he was pulling his car up to the curb in front of a compact Cape Cod style house in a quiet residential neighborhood. The small front lawn was littered with dead leaves from the maple, oak, and sycamore trees that flanked the walk. A small bicycle, metallic purple, with streamers dangling from the handlebars and training wheels attached to the frame, leaned against the side of the house. A willow wreath hung on the front door.

It wasn't a sprawling twelve-room Victorian overlooking the ocean. But then, Gwen wasn't a movie star who was paid obscene amounts of money to lead the Galaxy Force in combat against evil aliens.

Still, if Dylan had known he had a daughter—if that spitfire bitch had done him the courtesy of informing him of this fact—he would have bought them a bigger house with a more spacious yard.

His daughter. *His daughter.* Just thinking about it caused his emotions to spin like a tornado, a violent storm tearing apart everything in his world that had once been solid.

All right, so Gwen had kept this profound truth from him. That was the choice she'd made, and it allowed him to make his own choice. He could pretend he'd never seen that little girl who looked so much like his niece—who looked so freaking much like *him*. He could pretend he had no idea she existed. He could go on with his life, dating, hooking up, remaining open to the possibility that some woman would someday enter his life and steal his heart, and they could make a commitment and create children both of them knew about.

He couldn't live in Brogan's Point, though. That was for sure.

But he wanted to live in Brogan's Point. Not just because of the ocean view of the house he'd bid on, not just because the town was peaceful and tranquil and the sea breezes soothed his spirit more effectively than any drug known to humankind, but because...

Because he had a daughter. And that daughter was in this town. And damn it, he couldn't pretend he hadn't seen her. She existed. She *lived.* She colored pictures of someone or something named Mr. Snuffy. A piece of Dylan was walking the earth. A piece of his heart, a piece of his soul, was here in this town, in this world.

Christ. It was a tornado, all right, like the storms that swept across the plains of his Nebraska childhood, blowing everything in their path to smithereens. His life felt splintered, shattered. Unrecognizable. And it was all Gwendolyn Parker's fault.

***

At eleven a.m., the Faulk Street Tavern was pretty empty, which Dylan supposed was a good thing. He knew the joke about it being five o'clock somewhere, but he didn't really want anything alcoholic.

What he wanted was to confront Gwen, to grab her by the shoulders and shake her until her eyes dissolved in tears and she begged his forgiveness—or until she whipped out evidence that proved her daughter had nothing to do with him.

Sure. Just a coincidence that she'd have a daughter with Dylan's curly brown hair and dark brown eyes and pointy chin, whose age implied that she was born exactly nine months after Gwen and Dylan had spent a night jumping each other's bones.

He'd wanted to sit in the car by the curb, watching Gwen's house until she showed up. But stores stayed open late on Saturdays. Hours might pass before she left work. In those hours, some neighbor might grow suspicious of the nondescript rental car parked on the street, its occupant focused on Gwen's house like a crazed stalker.

He couldn't stomach the thought of returning to the Ocean Bluff Inn, or driving back to the Victorian he hoped to buy. He'd considered phoning his manager, but what would he say to Brian? *Congratulate me—I'm a daddy.* Brian would shit a brick.

So he'd gone to the Faulk Street Tavern instead. The place was nearly empty. A middle-aged guy in a ratty parka and baggy jeans sat alone on a stool at the far left end of the bar, hunched over a drink.

Another middle-aged man, better groomed and in better shape, also sat at the bar, his hands curved around a coffee mug as he chatted with the tall bartender with the reddish hair and the wry smile.

A mug of hot coffee sounded like a good idea. Straight up, no Irish or Jamaican. Just the real thing. The caffeine might supercharge his heart, but it would also clear his head. And his head definitely needed clearing.

He approached the bar. The well-groomed man twisted in his seat to acknowledge Dylan. "Hey, it's the actor!"

Dylan shrugged. He wasn't in the mood to make nice with a fan, but rudeness didn't suit him. "I guess the sunglasses and beard aren't much of a disguise."

"I've seen through much more elaborate disguises," the man said, extending his right hand. "Ed Nolan. I'm a detective with the Brogan's Point police department."

Dylan shook hands with Nolan. The guy's grip was strong, his palm warm from the mug he'd been holding. "I've never been able to grow a really thick beard," Dylan confessed. "I guess I'd better stay on the right side of the law."

"That would be a good policy," Nolan said. "Gus—" he tipped his head toward the bartender "—told me you were in town. I remember when you were here a few years back, making that movie about the boat."

"The local police were great while we were doing that shoot," Dylan recalled. They'd blocked off roads when necessary, and arranged with ship owners to allow for filming on one of the wharves. They'd helped with permits, directed traffic, and facilitated a night shoot on the high school's football field. "We couldn't have made that movie without you."

Nolan chuckled. "I guess if I ever get tired of police work, I can head out to Hollywood and make movies there."

"Yeah," the bartender said. "Or if they fire you for visiting a bar in the middle of the morning."

Nolan glanced at his watch and stood. "I'm entitled to my coffee break." He turned to Dylan. "Riley's is already too crowded with the early lunch crowd. And if I go to Dunkin or Starbucks, I'll wind up buying some pastry to go with the coffee." He patted his flat stomach. "Gotta watch my weight."

"Sure," the bartender teased. "Admit it, Ed—you just can't stay away from me."

"Got that right." Nolan drained his cup and passed it across the bar to her. "See you later, babe." He leaned across the bar and brushed her cheek with a kiss, and Dylan realized the bartender had been serious. They were a couple.

He wondered if they were married. If they had kids. If one of them would ever lie to the other the way Gwen had lied to Dylan.

The bartender watched Detective Nolan stroll across the room and out the door, then set his mug in a sink behind the bar. "Can I get you something?"

"Coffee, please." Dylan watched the door swing shut behind Nolan. From there, his gaze strayed to the jukebox standing against the wall. He studied its polished surface, the sleek arch of its dome, the vivid hues of the peacocks adorning its front panel.

The thunk of porcelain meeting wood prompted him to turn back to the bar, where a thick mug of steaming coffee sat before him. "Cream or sugar?" the bartender asked.

"No, this is fine." He took a sip, scalding his tongue. Not that he minded the beverage's heat. He needed to jolt his brain into functionality. Like those paddles doctors used to shock a heart back to life, the coffee shocked his mind. He took another sip.

The bartender sidled down the bar a few feet and got busy slicing lemons into thin yellow circles. Dylan watched her for a minute, waiting for the caffeine to kick in.

When he closed his eyes, he pictured that bubbly little girl scampering through the Attic, her curly hair frothing around her face and her giggle filling the air. So he kept his eyes open. He watched the silver blade of the bartender's knife slide through the lemon, again and again. He watched the guy down at the end of the bar droop over his drink, his chin nearly resting on his glass. Behind Dylan stood the jukebox, and he peered over his shoulder at it before taking another drink of coffee.

"When I was here yesterday evening," he called to the bartender, "the jukebox played a song."

Nodding, she reached for another lemon.

"It was...I mean..." His brain still didn't seem to be operating properly, because he heard himself say, "It was almost like it cast a spell on me or something."

Rather than laugh at him, or even look startled, the bartender nodded again.

What did that mean? Did she agree that the song had bewitched him? "It was weird. The song almost seemed familiar to me, even though I never heard it before."

"It was probably a hit when your mother was in grade school," the bartender said. "That jukebox plays only old songs. It plays records, not CD's or MP3's. Anything it plays had to have been popular when people listened to 45's."

He wasn't sure what she meant by a 45. He knew about 45's in the context of firearms—45-caliber handguns—but not in the context of music. Those single-song vinyl records, maybe?

He reflected on what had happened when the jukebox had played that 45 yesterday. He'd already spotted Gwen, but she hadn't seen him until the song began, that wistful ballad about a man leaving a woman. If the song hadn't played, would Gwen have continued chatting with her male companion, never noticing Dylan? If she hadn't noticed Dylan, would he have gone to her store this morning? If he hadn't gone into her store, would he have happily continued his life, never knowing about the little girl who looked like him?

Bewitched wasn't the right word. *Manipulated*, perhaps. It was because of the song that Gwen had locked eyes with him. Because of the song that he'd gone to the Attic. Because of the song that he'd seen the girl.

"Some folks think it's magic," the bartender said.

Her voice short-circuited his thoughts. "What's magic?"

"The jukebox. They claim it sometimes plays a song someone in the room has to hear."

"What do you mean?"

She scooped up the yellow wheels of sliced lemon and dropped them into a bowl, then tossed the knife into the sink and rinsed her hands. "They say the jukebox will play a song that changes the course of your life. Not always, but sometimes. Not for everyone, just for some people." She shot him a look, and that wry, enigmatic smile returned to her lips. "I saw you yesterday. You and Gwen Parker. That song was telling you something."

That she could articulate what he'd been thinking, what he'd been feeling, made it seem possible to him. "What was the song telling me?"

She shrugged. "That's for you to figure out. You and Gwen."

Dylan knew about magic. He knew that he could act out an entire scene with himself in front of a green screen, and CGI would add monsters and spaceships and constellations of stars—and magically, movie audiences would see Captain Steele battling aliens in deep space.

But a song? An old rock song about a man touching a woman's cheek and walking away?

Angel of the morning.

If that song was magic, he wished it had worked its magic so that Gwen *hadn't* seen him, so that he could have walked away from her and never had to think about her as anything more than someone with whom he'd shared a fun, meaningless night a long time ago. He wished the song could magically restore his life to the way it was before he'd seen his daughter.

Because, damn it, he couldn't walk away now.

Chapter Six

The afternoon flew by.

After lunch, Gwen took Annie to the supermarket to buy groceries. Annie loved going to the supermarket, pretending she was steering the automobile-shaped cart designed for children and making purchasing suggestions. "Cara says round waffles taste better than the square ones," she shouted up to Gwen from her position behind the steering wheel. "We should get round ones. Can we buy bread sticks? We need carrots! The little baby ones!"

Once they restocked the kitchen, they drove to Annie's friend Lucy's house for a play date. While Annie and Lucy spent two noisy hours attempting to dress Lucy's cocker spaniel in a sunhat and T-shirt and racing around the back yard with the tolerant pooch, Gwen sat in the kitchen with Lucy's mother, indulging in a glass of white wine and a significant amount of gossip. Gwen learned that the parents of Cara Schmidt—she of the round waffles—were getting a divorce, and that the principal at the girls' school had just received some sort of award from the state, and that Paul Hammond's mother was planning to invite the entire kindergarten class to Paul's birthday party in December. "She's nuts," Lucy's mother declared. Gwen had to agree. Twenty-two screeching, sugar-crazed five-year-olds in one house? Insane.

She appreciated the distraction Lucy and her mother provided. The gossip gave her something to think about besides Dylan Scott, his unwelcome intrusion in her life, and her fear that he'd intrude in Annie's life, as well.

But eventually the play date ended. Gwen buckled Annie into her car seat and they headed for home. By now, Gwen thought hopefully, Dylan might be halfway back to California. She didn't have to worry about him, did she? He'd bolted from the store as soon as he'd seen Annie. Surely he wanted nothing to do with Gwen's little girl.

"Can we get a dog?" Annie asked, her voice drifting forward from the back seat. Her cheeks were ruddy from romping outdoors with Lucy in the chilly, late-autumn afternoon. She'd probably fall asleep early tonight.

It wasn't the first time Annie had asked for a dog, nor the first time Gwen had to answer with a no. "It's hard to take care of a dog when no one's home all day," she said. "I work, and you're at school and then in the after-school program. Who'd play with the dog while we were gone? Who'd feed it and let it out to go to the bathroom?"

"I could stop going to after-school," Annie proposed. "I could come home and play with the dog."

"But then I'd have to hire a baby-sitter every day, and you wouldn't be able to play with your friends." The program Annie attended from three each afternoon until Gwen picked her up at around five cost significantly less than a nanny or au pair, and it offered Annie plenty of playmates and the opportunity to enjoy activities Gwen didn't want to deal with. She often joked with the other mothers that she'd enrolled Annie in the program solely so Annie wouldn't finger-paint at home. She could do her finger-painting at the after-school program, and Gwen's house would be spared that particular mess.

"I could bring the dog to after-school."

"We'll discuss getting a dog when you're a little older," Gwen promised. She'd had dogs growing up, but she'd also had an older brother, and her parents, both professors at the University of Illinois, had had flexible schedules, so there was always someone around to take care of the assorted Parker pets. She would love for Annie to have a dog, too—and maybe, if she and Mike got married, they could figure out a schedule that would allow for pet care.

Right now, though, Gwen had her hands full caring for Annie and the store. She couldn't take on any more responsibilities.

"Is Mike coming over tonight?" Annie asked as Gwen steered up the driveway and pushed the remote to open the garage.

"Probably." But possibly not. He'd been pissed off yesterday, because despite Gwen's having hired a baby-sitter, freeing her for the evening, she and Mike hadn't wound up making love. She'd been too upset about having seen Dylan at the Faulk Street Tavern, and she hadn't been able to tell Mike the cause of her distress. What should she have said to him? "There's the father of my daughter." No, that wouldn't have been good.

She and Mike had been dating a year before she'd finally felt comfortable enough to tell him that Annie's father had been a member of the film crew that had passed through town six years ago. Mike hadn't pressed for more information, and she hadn't offered any. If she'd revealed to Mike that Dylan Scott—Captain Steele himself—had contributed the sperm that created Annie, Mike would be pestering her to hire a lawyer and take Dylan for every dollar she could wring out of him. That was the way Mike was.

She might be thinking about marrying him, but certain things were her own business. Annie would undoubtedly benefit from having a father figure in her life, but while Mike might pass as a father figure, he would never be Annie's father. Gwen had raised her little girl single-handedly, and she wasn't about to trust Mike Bonneville or anyone else to step in and take over.

Sometimes she thought her reluctance to allow Mike full parenting privileges was a sign that she didn't really love him enough to marry him. But she was well past believing that some ideal man would magically sweep into her world and make it complete, that he'd not only love Annie as much as Gwen did but he'd share her child-rearing philosophy and fill every crack and pit in her life like warm putty, smoothing all the rough spots.

Mike was a good man. Gwen got along with him, and he wanted to marry her. She'd reached the point in her life when stability and comfort seemed more important than romance.

Nothing's perfect, she reminded herself as she and Annie entered the house. They hooked their coats on the wall pegs in the mudroom and continued into the kitchen. Gwen checked her phone to see if Mike had left a message. He hadn't. She'd make enough dinner for him, and if he didn't come, she'd freeze the leftovers. He wasn't crazy about her spaghetti and meat sauce, anyway, since she used whole-wheat pasta and ground turkey, along with stewed tomatoes, mushrooms, broccoli and whatever other vegetables she felt like tossing in. "Too healthy," Mike would complain. If he could eat pizza three times a day, he'd be a happy man.

Annie donned her apron. She was always eager to help Gwen cook. Sometimes Gwen thought this was mainly because she loved the apron, with its pictures of Winnie-the-Pooh characters adorning it and its long waist strings that she could wrap around her wiry little body and tie in front. At her age, she was mostly tasked with mixing things, stirring things, and setting the table—nothing involving sharp knives or stove burners—but Gwen was grateful they could share this time.

Annie was tearing romaine into the salad bowl and Gwen was sautéing the vegetables and ground turkey when the doorbell rang. "Mike!" Annie shouted, jumping down from the step-stool she used to reach the counter and darting out of the kitchen.

Gwen turned off the stove and followed Annie to the front door. "Let me answer," she warned Annie, but her daughter was already swinging the door open. That was something Gwen needed to work with her on. Annie was too short to see out the window in the upper part of the door; she had to learn not to open it when she didn't know who was on the other side.

In this case, the person on the other side wasn't Mike. It was Dylan Scott.

Annie fell back a step, although she didn't look alarmed. "Mommy, it's a customer," she said. "From the store."

She had a good memory. Then again, Dylan was pretty unforgettable.

Gwen's stomach clenched. It was one thing for him to locate her store on Seaview Avenue—he'd been there six years ago, after all—but another for him to locate her house. And another yet for him not just to locate her house but to stand on her porch, feet firmly planted on the bricks, one hand gripping the door frame, as if he expected her to shove him down the steps. A shove wouldn't get rid of him, she knew. He looked immovable.

He also looked angry.

And ridiculously sexy, with his wild hair and his scruff of beard and that sinfully macho leather jacket.

Gwen gave her daughter a gentle nudge. "Annie, sweetheart, would you go in the kitchen, please?"

"Is he staying for dinner?" Annie asked.

"No," Gwen said quickly, aware that Dylan had been about to speak. His mouth remained half-open, his lips sliding into a humorless grin. "Please go in the kitchen while I talk to Mr. Scott."

Annie peered up at him, her eyes wide. He stared right back at her, and Gwen suppressed a shudder as their resemblance registered on her. Did Annie sense the connection? Could she tell, just by looking at Dylan, that he was her father?

"Annie?"

"Okay," Annie said reluctantly, tearing her gaze from Dylan and clomping back to the kitchen.

"She likes me," Dylan said.

Gwen pressed her lips together. Until she figured out how to deal with him, her safest strategy was to remain silent.

"Can I come in?"

"No."

His smile disappeared. He spoke softly, urgently, an undertone of bitterness stretching his voice taut. "Look. You went and had this child.

You never told me about her. You kept this a secret from me. Damn it, Gwen—"

"I did *not* keep her a secret from you. I contacted you half a dozen times. You didn't want any part of her—or me. So please, just leave us alone."

"What the hell are you talking about?" Rage seethed beneath the surface of his steady voice, threatening to bubble over.

"Mommy?" Annie's voice floated in from the kitchen. "I'm done with the lettuce."

Gwen was torn in two. Half of her wanted to return to the kitchen, to resume preparing dinner with Annie—to go back to the life she'd been living before a song had burst out of the Faulk Street Tavern jukebox and changed everything. The other half of her wanted to remain in the front hall, just across the threshold from Dylan. She wanted to dive into his dark eyes, to discover what lay behind them. Was he lying? Was he insane? Did he really not know what she was talking about? At this point, did it matter?

"I have to go," she said, then eased the door shut and let out a long breath. His eyes... They truly were mesmerizing.

She couldn't let her thoughts veer off in that direction. He had come to her house to discuss the daughter whose existence he'd decided, years ago, to ignore. It was too late. There was no room in her life, or Annie's, for an irresponsible asshole like Dylan Scott, regardless of how mesmerizing his eyes were.

She hurried back down the hall to the kitchen, where she found Annie pulling a tub of pitted olives from a low shelf in the refrigerator. "Can I put olives in the salad?" she asked.

"Yes, but not like last time." A few days ago, Annie had emptied the entire tub—a good two dozen olives—into a salad just for the two of them. "Can you count out ten olives?"

"I can count to a hundred," Annie boasted, giving her mother a long-suffering look. "I can count to a skillion."

"Well, we don't want a skillion olives in the salad. Or even a hundred olives. Just put in ten."

"I'll put in twelve," Annie announced. Sometimes the girl's stubbornness drove Gwen up a wall. Other times, though, it filled her with pride. After all, she'd inherited that stubbornness from her mother.

The doorbell rang again. "Don't answer it," Gwen warned, but Annie was already prancing down the hall, still clutching the plastic tub containing the olives. Gwen raced after her. "Remember what I said about not opening the door when you don't know who's on the other side?"

"I do know," Annie said, although she obediently refrained from twisting the door knob. "It's Mike."

Gwen peered through the window embedded in the door. She saw Mike. "Well, you're right this time," she told Annie. "You can let him in."

Smiling, Annie swung open the door. Mike stood on the porch—but so did Dylan. He'd been just beyond Gwen's sight-line when she'd glanced out the window.

He and Mike were already bonding, unfortunately. "Look who I found on your doorstep," Mike said, stepping inside and planting a friendly kiss on Gwen's cheek. "A famous actor!"

Annie gazed up at Dylan. "Are you famous?" she asked.

"He's an actor," Gwen said before Dylan could answer. "Annie, please go to the kitchen."

"I want to say hi to Mike."

"Say hi, and then go to the kitchen."

Annie looked irritated. Mike looked bemused. Dylan looked...angry and sexy, like before. He also looked as if he understood why she wanted Annie far away.

"Hi," Annie grumbled. "Mommy's making spaghetti with lots of vegetables. You won't like it."

Mike laughed. He must have stopped home after work before coming here. He never wore jeans to work—"No one wants to buy a new car from someone wearing jeans," he claimed—but he was wearing them now, along with sneakers, a New England Patriots sweatshirt and a lined windbreaker. "I can pick out the vegetables," he said. "So, Annie, did you know this is a movie star? He's Captain Steele, from the Galaxy Force movies."

"She hasn't seen those movies," Gwen said. "She's too young."

"I could see them," Annie said, her gaze still fixed on Dylan. "I'm big now. I go to school."

"In a couple of years," Gwen said, trying to sound reasonable. "There's lots of violence in them. Guns and explosions." She shot Mike a sharp look. Thanks to him—and Dylan—she'd been forced to make a second in-the-future promise to Annie: a dog, and now Dylan's stupid movies. "Mike, why don't you help Annie with the salad? I have to talk to Dylan."

Mike's eyebrows twitched up and down, but he was smiling as he took the tub of olives from Annie. "Come on, Annie-girl. Let's make a salad."

"I already did the lettuce," she told him as they headed down the hall together.

As soon as they were gone, Gwen turned back to Dylan. He still stood on the porch—and still looked as if he'd rooted himself there and had no intention of going anywhere.

At least he hadn't entered the house. Gwen positioned herself in the doorway so he'd have to knock her over if he wanted to come inside. He might be angry, but she doubted he would tackle her just to get to Annie.

"So—he's not your husband," he said, angling his head in the direction Mike had disappeared.

"No." Gwen didn't owe him an explanation about her love life, but it was easier to answer that simple question than to argue.

"Gwen." He sounded a little calmer than he had before. "You never told me you were pregnant. If you had, I would have..." He mulled over his words, then concluded, "Done something. Helped you out. Made arrangements."

"I did tell you. I found your contact information on a website and sent several emails. I did research and phoned your management company."

He frowned. "You told them you were pregnant?"

"I told them I had important information and I needed to speak with you. I wasn't even sure at first if I was going to terminate the pregnancy. I wanted to talk to you before I made that decision."

His forehead creased with a frown. He glanced up at the sky, then shook his head. "You should have told them you were pregnant. They would have made sure I knew."

She snorted. "I did, finally. I didn't want to share something that personal with some receptionist in California, but when I didn't hear from you, I told her. She put me through to some man who told me to leave you alone. He said that if I tried to contact you again, he'd have me charged with harassment." At the time, she'd been shocked by the man's threat, and fearful. Now she felt only a low-burning resentment. "Needless to say, I didn't try to contact you again."

"Shit." He closed his eyes and shook his head again. "Gwen, I—"

"I decided not to get an abortion, and it was the right decision for me. And I'm perfectly content to leave you alone. I hope you'll return the favor. Annie doesn't need you in her life."

"Why? Because she's got that guy who isn't your husband? What's he, her substitute daddy?"

"None of your business," Gwen snapped. "Please. Just go."

He pondered her for a long moment, then relented. "I'll go. But I'll be back." With that promise—that threat—he turned and strode down the front walk, into the night.

Chapter Seven

"Dylan! It's about time you got back to me. I've been trying to reach you to discuss the licensing deal for that new Galaxy Force app. They want to use your likeness in the game. The numbers they've mentioned are excellent. We're still negotiating, but—"

"That's not why I'm calling," Dylan said. He was standing by the open window in his room at the Ocean Bluff Inn, a cold, salty breeze whispering through the screen. He could see pale gray wisps of clouds floating in the late evening sky above a dark ocean. The horizon was barely visible, dark blue against dark blue.

That darkness suited his mood. He'd turned on the desk lamp, but it spread only a small pool of amber light across the desk's surface, not much brighter than a night-light. He remained at the window, his back to the room, staring out at the night.

He didn't want to hear about Brian's negotiations regarding some cell-phone game that would feature a Captain Steele avatar who resembled Dylan about as much as Goofy resembled an actual dog, but which would wind up paying Dylan enough to make the house just a few minutes' drive north of where he stood even more affordable. It was ridiculous, the amount of money people flung at you when you were the star of a successful film franchise

He'd already heard back from Andrea with a counter-offer from the house's current owners; those negotiations were going fine. He wished he cared. Right now, he wasn't sure whether he should pay whatever the sellers demanded just to own that house in Brogan's Point, or pack up his stuff, return to California, and pretend he'd never set foot in this God-forsaken town.

But first things first. Brian. "I'm firing you," he said.

Brian fell silent for a moment. Then he burst into laughter, hoarse and rasping, a tribute to his thirty-year love affair with cigarettes. "Oh, come on, Dylan. You spend a few days on the East Coast and forget who you are! Look, I'm sorry *The Angel* didn't pan out. But I got you that audition, and they loved you. They didn't even want to consider you—they kept saying you couldn't possibly overcome your Captain Steele identity for the film. But I got you in the door, and you blew them away at the audition. You came this close to getting the part, man. I'm sorry I couldn't work a miracle for you, but I got you in front of them, and they thought you were fabulous."

"Screw that." Dylan dropped his gaze from the ocean outside to the glass in his hand. It contained an inch of scotch and a couple of ice cubes. They clinked against the glass as he took a sip. "Six years ago, I knocked a woman up."

Another silence. Then Brian said, "Okay, buddy. Personal business. I didn't know."

"*I* didn't know, either, until today. But I should have known. You ran interference. The woman tried to tell me at the time, and you stopped her."

"Six years ago? I have no memory of this."

"Well, she has more than a memory. She's got a little girl. *My daughter*. She said she tried repeatedly to contact me at the time, to let me know, and she finally got as far as you, and you threatened to have her arrested for harassment if she called again."

"Oh, man." Brian's sigh was loud, whistling through the phone. "Okay. This must have been right after the first Galaxy Force movie came out. It was crazy times, Dylan. You were suddenly a star, a fantasy stud. You were getting hundreds of calls and emails a day from women. They wanted you. They wanted to bed you. They wanted to own you. They knew you when you were eight years old. They went to college with you. At least a dozen of them claimed they were carrying your baby. They were crawling out of the woodwork, oozing out from under rocks. I had to protect you, Dylan. That's what you were paying me to do, and I did it."

Dylan said nothing. In the first few months after his debut as Captain Steele, he'd been heralded as cinema's newest hot guy. His privacy had evaporated; his face had appeared on celebrity websites, accompanied by stories of dubious origin. One supermarket tabloid had published a photo of him hugging his sister Grace—God knew where they'd gotten it—with a huge headline: *Captain Steele's Mystery Babe!*

The gorgeous little movie he'd filmed in Brogan's Point, *Sea Glass*, went forgotten. Dylan was Captain Steele. A star. The stuff of women's fantasies.

He'd been vaguely aware of all that Hollywood noise. He'd wanted to tune it out, and he had—thanks to Brian. His manager had run interference, and Dylan had let him.

"You're not going to fire me, okay?" Brian went on. "We've been through a lot together. I've made you rich, and you've made me rich. I'm sorry *The Angel* didn't work out, but I'll get you more auditions. You won't be Captain Steele forever. Once you finish your contract obligations to the Galaxy Force series, you can write your own ticket. *I'll* write your ticket for you, so it'll say exactly what you want it to say. Don't throw away a terrific partnership just because six years ago I did what you were paying me to do."

Another gulp of scotch couldn't wash away the truth in Brian's words. Brian had only been doing his job, protecting Dylan from his voracious new fans. Acknowledging that fact didn't make Dylan feel any better, however.

"So...this baby mama. What's the deal? Do we need to take care of her? Does she want money? How do you want me to handle this?"

"I *don't* want you to handle it." Brian may have done what Dylan had wanted him to do six years ago, but that didn't mean he'd done the right thing. "I've got a daughter."

"Yeah. Wow."

"I have to make things right," Dylan continued, talking to himself as much as to Brian. "I have to fix this."

"I'm your fixer, man. Tell me what you want me to do."

"Nothing," Dylan said. "Just be grateful I'm not firing you. Yet."

"It'll all work out, buddy," Brian promised him. "You're a good man. You'll do the right thing. Just let me know if I can help in any way."

How Brian could help was beyond Dylan. The man had no children of his own. He couldn't begin to understand the tangle of emotions settling in Dylan's gut like a knotted ball of yarn spun out of lead. Heavy, painful, impossible to unravel.

He said good-bye, disconnected the call, and took another slug of scotch. And struggled to unravel those knots, to smooth out that leaden thread of yarn.

First of all, financial obligations. Of course he'd pay child support.

But did he want to be that little girl's father? A *real* father, one who didn't just write checks but participated actively in her life. Gwen didn't want that. She'd already cast another guy in that role. Dylan had never even been granted an audition for it.

What did he know about being a father? He was a doting uncle, sure—but being an uncle was easy. You could spoil your nieces and nephews all you wanted, and accept none of the responsibility for them. He adored his sisters' kids, loved hanging out with them, loved family get-togethers when he could play catch with them or build architectural wonders out of Legos with them or give them piggy-back rides.

But a family gathering was one thing. Day in and day out, disciplining a daughter, signing permission slips from school, sitting up at night with her when she had an ear infection, arranging his schedule—his freaking *life*—around a child? Did he want that? Even if he did, could he do it?

Gwen had been doing it for five years now. All by herself. That just wasn't right.

And letting some other guy step in and take over Dylan's role... That wasn't right, either.

He polished off his drink and returned his gaze to the dark seascape on the other side of the window. And realized his mind was made up.

Chapter Eight

At some point in the future, Gwen believed, Sundays would be her sleep-late days. The Attic didn't open until noon, and even then, although she was on call in case an emergency cropped up, she usually took Sundays off. That was her prerogative as the boss. She felt comfortable leaving her capable staff in charge of the store in her absence.

But while she didn't have to put in time at the shop on Sundays, she didn't get to sleep late. Annie still believed that as soon as the sun rose, so could she—and she was a lot noisier than the sun.

By seven-thirty, Annie had abandoned the culinary masterpiece she'd been pretending to make in her toy kitchen for a real breakfast of waffles—the round ones, of course. Gwen wondered if they really tasted better than the square ones, but she wasn't curious enough to eat one herself. A cup of coffee and a toasted English muffin were all she could manage.

Sipping her coffee, she did her best to ignore the congealing drips of maple syrup on the table, the waffle crumb glued to Annie's chin, the mysterious pink smear marking Annie's pajama top. At least it wasn't finger-paint, Gwen acknowledged with a sigh.

She probably ought to run a load of laundry today. But Annie was babbling about some new movie Gwen had never heard of, a just-released animated feature about a singing kite, or maybe a singing cat. Gwen supposed she could take Annie to see that today. Maybe one of Annie's friends would join them, Cara or Lucy. After breakfast, Gwen would look up the show times and make a few phone calls.

She was tired—she was always tired; it came with the territory—but not as tired as she would have been if Mike had stayed over. She felt a little guilty that she'd sent him home after dinner, and even more guilty that she'd been relieved to see him go.

Even though they'd been dating more than a year, and Mike had raised the subject of marriage, she still felt uncomfortable having him in her bed when Annie was asleep just across the hall. Mothers were allowed to have sex, Gwen reminded herself. But on the rare occasions she and Mike made love in her house, she was always anxious about whether Annie would see him there, and she invariably hustled him out the door before Annie woke in the morning. Since Annie rose with the sun, this meant Mike had to leave while it was still dark. One time, he'd overslept, and Annie had been mystified to find him staggering out of the bathroom early Sunday morning. "Did you have a sleepover?" she'd asked.

Mike had thought this was hilarious. For the next few weeks, he'd kept asking Gwen if she was up for a pajama party. She hadn't been amused.

There had been no possibility of a pajama party last night, anyway. She'd been even more unsettled by Dylan Scott's presence on her front porch than she'd been the day before, by his presence at the Faulk Street Tavern. Even as she finished preparing dinner, as she tried to make conversation with Mike and Annie, as she kept Annie's sippy cup filled with milk and laughed off Mike's grousing about how much better *real* pasta tasted than the whole-grain stuff she insisted on serving, that song, "Angel of the Morning," kept echoing inside her head.

Touch my cheek before you leave.

Dylan hadn't touched her cheek. She was pretty sure he hadn't left, either. He might have walked away from her house last night, but he was still here somehow, his presence reverberating in the air.

That was the real reason Gwen felt guilty about having sent Mike home last night: she was preoccupied with thoughts of Dylan. Thoughts of what he wanted with her, what he wanted with Annie, whether he was going to force his way into their lives five-plus years too late. Thoughts of his penetrating gaze, his lean, lanky body, his beautiful mouth. Unwelcome memories of how that mouth had once felt pressed to hers, grazing across her skin, making every cell in her body sing with yearning.

So she wasn't entirely shocked when the doorbell rang as she was washing a gooey patch of syrup from Annie's hair. She wasn't angry when, despite her warning, Annie leaped down from the step-stool and raced to the front door. At least Annie didn't twist the door knob once she'd reached the entry hall. She stood waiting for Gwen's permission to open the door.

Gwen peered through the window. She wasn't the least bit surprised to see Dylan on the porch.

She was going to have to deal with him. He knew the truth about Annie, and he'd chosen not to run away from it. So this meeting was inevitable. She might as well get it over with.

She wished she was wearing something other than a pair of ratty jeans, a faded flannel shirt, and fleece slippers, though. She wished her nails were polished and her hair wasn't tied back in a sloppy pony-tail. Not that she needed to look good for Dylan, but he *was* a movie star, after all.

He hadn't exactly gone all out in his grooming, either. The jeans he had on might have been the same pair he'd worn yesterday, and she recognized his slouchy leather jacket. He looked as if he'd shaved, however. She saw the smooth, sharp lines of his jaw and remembered how his face had felt when she'd cupped her hands to his cheeks, when she'd kissed him so many years ago.

A dark shudder rippled through her. She didn't want to remember, but she couldn't seem to help herself.

He wasn't scowling today, and he'd come bearing gifts. One fist hand held a bouquet of autumn flowers—tan and golden and russet chrysanthemums—and the other held a book. He smiled tentatively, handed the flowers to Gwen, and said, "Can we start all over?"

She reluctantly took the bouquet. Accepting it represented something significant: that she was accepting Dylan, that she was willing to let him into her world. She reminded herself that when it came to her world, he had legal rights—to say nothing of biological rights. But the one night they'd spent together notwithstanding, he was a total stranger, an alien from the distant planet of Hollywood, and she didn't want him disturbing the balanced, placid life she'd established for herself and Annie.

He had already disturbed it. Nothing felt balanced or placid in his presence. Nothing felt normal, not even her heartbeat, her pulse thrumming inside her ears.

If he hadn't appeared at the tavern the other evening, and that song hadn't played, everything would be fine between Gwen and Mike. They would have made love Friday—and maybe even last night. They could have had a pajama party.

Nothing felt fine between them now. She couldn't even think of having sex with Mike when Dylan kept showing up. He'd thrown everything out of whack. A pretty bouquet of mums wouldn't change that.

"This is for Annie," he said, showing the book to Gwen. *Now We Are Six*, by A.A. Milne. "She had that apron on yesterday, with the Winnie-the-Pooh characters. And I figure she's smart enough to handle poems for six-year-olds, even if she's only five. Is it okay if I give it to her?"

Gwen appreciated his checking with her before he presented the book to Annie. She nodded. "How did you find a bookstore open this early on a Sunday morning?"

"I ordered it on-line and had it overnighted," he said.

She supposed that when you were a movie star, you could do things like that. If necessary, you could hire a private jet to fly the book to your doorstep. That he could get a book less than twenty-four hours after ordering it was just more evidence that he was from an alternate universe.

Yet how could she resent him? Not only had he asked her permission to give Annie the book, but he'd noticed the characters on Annie's apron last night.

Annie eagerly accepted the book and started flipping through the pages. "I can read," she bragged. "I'm in kindergarten."

Her reading skills weren't exactly in the genius range, but she could probably get through some of the poems. Gwen cleared her throat and gave Annie's shoulder a gentle nudge.

"Thank you," Annie dutifully said, craning her neck to gaze up at Dylan. The resemblance between the two struck Gwen like a fist to the gut.

Gwen steered her attention back to Dylan. "Do you want something to eat? I made Annie some frozen waffles—"

"The round kind," Annie added.

"No, thanks," he said, his voice soft, hesitant. "I had breakfast at the inn."

"Some coffee, then?" He'd given her these beautiful flowers. She owed him at least that much.

"That sounds great."

"Annie, Mr. Scott and I need to talk. If you'd like, you can go downstairs and play." She knew that if Annie returned to the playroom in the finished basement, she would wind up either watching TV or playing a computer game on her tablet. Gwen tried to limit Annie's screen time, but right now she and Dylan needed a few uninterrupted minutes to discuss their situation. When Annie let out a gleeful yelp and scampered down the hall to the stairs, Gwen told herself a half-hour of cartoons or computer games wouldn't damage her daughter too terribly.

Still, apprehension nibbled at her—apprehension about Dylan. Would he make demands? Accuse her of being a bad mother? Insinuate himself into her and Annie's lives?

He'd already insinuated himself. Whatever else they had to deal with, it couldn't be avoided. He was here. She might as well find how bad this was going to be.

Suppressing a sigh, she led Dylan to the kitchen. Having him inside her home unnerved her. If she were able to be objective about this, she'd be tickled to think she had a major movie star in her house, walking down her hall, standing in the middle of her kitchen. It was in need of renovation but she didn't have the money for that. What must he think of the twenty-five-year-old linoleum tiles on the floor, the Formica counters, the coiled electric burners on her exceedingly non-gourmet stove top?

At least the room wasn't too messy. She gathered the dirty plates from the table, dumped them in the sink, then busied herself preparing a fresh pot of coffee. Behind her, she heard the quiet rustle of Dylan removing his jacket. She glanced around in time to see him drape it over the back of a chair. He moved to the window overlooking the back yard. A cardinal was helping itself to a feast at the bird-feeder on the other side of the glass. Gwen and Annie loved watching the birds come and go, and in the summer she kept several feeders filled. But with the colder weather, only the die-hard year-rounders stopped by to binge on the birdseed she left for them.

The coffee maker gurgled. She found a vase and filled it with water, then stuffed the flowers into it, unsure of how she was supposed to feel about them. They weren't the gift of a lover. He'd apologized when he'd handed them to her—but they didn't make her feel any better about his having shunned her six years ago, when she'd tried to inform him she was pregnant. A bunch of chrysanthemums, no matter how pretty, didn't make up for that.

She carried the sugar bowl to the table, and a clean teaspoon. As a movie star, he might be accustomed to cream in his coffee, but she didn't have any. He'd have to make do with milk.

Slumming in Brogan's Point, she thought with a wry smile. What would his celebrity friends think?

When the coffee was done brewing, she refilled her cup, filled a fresh mug for him, and took a seat at the table. He settled into a chair across from her and watched her stir some milk into her coffee. When she nudged the pitcher toward him, he held up his hand and shook his head. Neither of them spoke.

The silence compelled Gwen to look at him. He returned her gaze, his eyes as dark as the coffee in his mug. As an actor, he knew how to convey emotions with those eyes, but right now they were opaque. Gwen couldn't begin to guess what he was thinking.

"I talked to my manager last night," he said. "I came close to firing him."

She waited.

"He said that when you contacted me... I guess lots of women were trying to contact me then, right after the first Galaxy Force movie came out. They were all claiming they carried my baby. My manager figured you were just one more crazed fan."

No, I wasn't just one more crazed fan. No point in saying that. She sipped her coffee.

"I'm really sorry, Gwen. I mean—I'm not the kind of guy who doesn't take responsibility for things. I'm a nice boy from Nebraska, right?"

He flashed her a quick, breathtaking smile. She remembered sitting with him at the Faulk Street Tavern so many years ago, sharing memories of their Midwestern childhoods. He'd been so easy to talk to, so unaffected, so unpretentious. He'd told her he was a small-town kid. His grandparents and uncle were farmers, but his parents had moved to the big city—a speck of a town just a few miles from the family farm. His father had been a plumber, his mother the receptionist for the town doctor. Over dinner, he'd hear about everyone who was sick in town, and everyone whose toilets had backed up. He used to bicycle to the farm in the summer, to help his grandparents out. He'd loved hiding in the rows of corn, pretending he was a prisoner of war—a very clever one, who could sneak through the maze of stalks to freedom. Or he'd pretend the main barn was a ship and he was a sea captain. Farms were wonderful places for playing make-believe, he'd told her. He hadn't realized he was an actor until he'd gotten to high school and his English teacher, desperate for boys to appear in the school's production of Romeo and Juliet, had cajoled him into trying out. He'd won the part of Romeo, and he'd been hooked.

Sitting with him in her kitchen, in the golden glow of the morning light spilling through the window, she recalled that conversation as if they'd had it mere days ago. She remembered thinking, as he'd told her about his evolution from small-town kid to professional actor, that he must have been type-cast as Romeo. He'd been so handsome, so charismatic. If she'd been a fourteen-year-old Juliet, she would have dumped her fiancé and swallowed poison for Dylan.

They'd talked, and they'd danced. She couldn't recall what songs the jukebox had played that evening, although she was positive "Angel of the Morning" wasn't among them. She and Dylan had danced fast and they'd danced slow. She'd drunk wine and he'd drunk beer, but neither of them got tipsy. Just...loose. Comfortable. Easy with each other.

She remembered one dance—not the song but the moment, the movement. Her arms had rested on his shoulders, his hands had curved around her waist. They'd looked into each other's eyes and shared the same thought. And then they'd kissed. Just a light kiss, a friendly kiss. A kiss shimmering with promise.

She'd barely known him, but she'd known she wanted to be with him. He'd made her feel desirable again, after Adam had left her. He'd made her feel womanly. Sensual. Sexy.

She gazed at his hands, cupped around the mug. They were still big but graceful, his fingers long and strong. She could almost imagine their warm grip, one on each side of her waist, just above her hips, holding her as they danced. She'd lifted her hands to his cheeks that night, and drawn his mouth to hers on the dance floor in the Faulk Street Tavern. So many years ago.

That kiss had completely altered the course of Gwen's life. It had led to Annie.

"She seems like a great kid," Dylan said, yanking Gwen back to the present.

"Annie? Yes. She's wonderful."

"Smart. Happy. You must be a terrific mother."

She shrugged. "I do my best."

"All by yourself." He shook his head. "Do you have any family around to help out?"

"They're all still in Illinois," she told him. "But I've got babysitters, and Annie's in school now. Full-day kindergarten and an after-school program which she really enjoys."

"And your boyfriend," Dylan added. "I guess he helps out, too."

Gwen shrugged again. Mike got along well enough with Annie, although Gwen believed Annie was more attached to him than he was to her. His affection for Annie seemed mostly about pleasing Gwen, doing what he knew she wanted him to do. She appreciated his effort, but that was what it was: an effort. It didn't come naturally to him.

Before Dylan had appeared in Brogan's Point, Mike's effort had been enough. It probably still was enough.

But Dylan had come and disrupted everything. "What exactly do you want?" she asked him, then winced inwardly at how cold and demanding she sounded.

"I want to be Annie's father," he said.

Blunt, and in a way just as cold and demanding. "How do you propose to do that? She lives in Brogan's Point. You live in California."

"I'm thinking of buying a house here in town," he told her.

That news stunned her into silence for a moment. "Really? You saw her and decided to uproot yourself and move here, just like that?"

"Actually, no." He drank some coffee, then leaned back in his chair. Evidently, he was feeling more comfortable. Gwen wasn't sure she liked that. "The reason I came here was to buy a house. I liked this town when we were filming *Sea Glass*. And I was getting restless in Los Angeles. It just wasn't feeling right to me."

She sensed there was more to his decision than things just not feeling right, but she didn't press him. She didn't want to know. His business was his business. She only wished he'd stay out of her business. Hers and Annie's.

"I had good memories of Brogan's Point," he told her. "I loved the ocean, the town. The people." His gaze grew more intense. "You were part of those memories, Gwen. Not that...I mean, it wasn't like I've been, you know, dreaming about you all these years..."

Certainly not. She'd seen plenty of photos of him with this or that beautiful actress on the covers of the magazines at the supermarket checkout.

"It was a good time, that night," he said.

She appreciated his unadorned honesty, and she couldn't argue with him. The night they'd spent together had been pretty spectacular.

"It just didn't..." He tapped his fingers against the surface of the table. "I didn't know about the unintended consequences. We used condoms, didn't we?"

"They aren't fool-proof," she pointed out.

"Obviously." A wry laugh escaped him. "So. Look. I hope we can figure this out in a way that will work for both of us. I don't want to screw up what you've got going here. But if I move into town, I want to be a part of Annie's life. I feel like I've already missed so much."

He'd missed the sleepless newborn nights. The messy diapers. The Terrible Two's and the threenager year. The stomach viruses. The demands for round waffles and dogs and movies about singing kites.

The nights when Gwen was bone-tired from a long day at work and all she wanted was a glass of wine and an hour of peace, and Annie was revved up and bouncing off the walls.

He'd also missed her giggles. Her hugs. Her sticky kisses. Her pride when she began to pick out words in the pages of her books and sound them out. "That says *dog*. That says *car*." He'd missed the pictures she drew, of Mr. Snuffy and the oak tree in the back yard, and the birds at the feeder. He'd missed her preschool graduation ceremony, and the first time at the Community Center pool when she'd stuck her face in the water and blown bubbles, and then bobbed back up, smiling as if she'd conquered Mt. Everest. He'd missed her cuddling up in the crook of his arm and murmuring, "I love you."

Gwen wasn't sure she wanted to share Annie with Mike. She definitely wasn't sure she wanted to share her with Dylan Scott.

But what was the alternative? To deny him access to Annie? She was his daughter. His blood.

Besides, he had money. He could hire a battalion of lawyers if Gwen tried to fight him.

She didn't want to fight him, anyway. She had nothing against him. The night they'd spent together so long ago had been lovely.

"So, you're going to move to town, and...what? Give up your film career? I can't offer you a job in my store."

He chuckled. "I'm still acting," he said, his gaze drifting toward the window for a moment, as a second cardinal joined the first at the feeder. "I'm under contract to do three more Galaxy Force movies in the next three years, and who knows what else. But I don't have to live in Hollywood to do that. I can get on a plane and fly wherever we're filming."

"Beyond the Milky Way?" she asked, quoting a tag line from the advertisements for the movies.

He laughed again. He had a disarming laugh, low and throaty. "Mostly on a massive sound stage in Vancouver." His smile faded. "Does Annie know I'm her father?"

"No."

"She must ask, though. Doesn't she wonder who her father is?"

His voice was edged in doubt and suspicion. Did he think Gwen had lied to Annie about who her father was? "She's never asked who," she said. "She's asked if she had a father, and I told her she did. She asked where he was, and I told her he lived far away. I told her that maybe she'd meet him someday. I guess it didn't seem odd to her. Some of her classmates are in single-parent families. Some have step-parents. One of her closest friends has two mommies."

He mulled over her words. "I guess you know better than me how to handle this."

Oh, sure. Gwen had no idea how to handle it. But then, she'd had no idea how to handle single motherhood, until she'd been forced to. Somehow, she'd figured it out. She supposed she would figure out how to introduce Dylan into Annie's life, too. One step, one day, one book at a time.

She'd figure it out, because she had no choice.

Chapter Nine

Dylan might be a creature of the film industry, but children's movies were not his area of expertise. He'd been approached once to do a voice in a Pixar film, but the job had conflicted with his Galaxy Force obligations, so he'd had to pass. He knew and admired folks who worked on animated features, but liking them didn't mean he was obligated to sit through their movies, so he skipped them.

Sky High wasn't bad, though. The story, which had something to do with a little girl who sailed through the air on a magic kite, was loud and colorful, with the sort of catchy songs that threatened to lodge permanently inside his skull. The theater in the multiplex was noisy with the babble of the dozens of children in the audience, and the air was dense with the cloying aroma of popcorn.

Gwen had allowed Annie to sit between Dylan and herself. Maybe he was reading too much into that, but he viewed the seating arrangement as an indication of trust. She wouldn't stand between him and his daughter—or sit between them at the movies.

Annie clearly found the movie enthralling. He'd bought her a small popcorn—movie-theater small, which meant the tub was almost as big as her head and he'd wound up eating more than half. His tongue felt greasy, and salt caked the corners of his mouth. But sharing popcorn with Annie struck him as a very father-daughter thing to do.

He needed to remind himself that fatherhood was a lot more complicated, and a lot more challenging, than simply taking his daughter to a kiddie matinee and munching on popcorn with her. In the movie's few scary scenes, she invariably leaned into Gwen's shoulder and squeezed Gwen's hand. Dylan was not the person she'd turn to when she was afraid.

Not yet.

Hell. What did he know about being a father, anyway? He'd watched enough sit-coms as a kid to know there were two kinds of fathers: the wise, steady fathers popular in the black-and-white shows from the fifties and sixties in perpetual reruns on TV Land, and the incompetent, goofball fathers popular in the shows from his own childhood. He would much rather be the first kind of father, but wise? Steady? Those weren't exactly words he'd use to describe himself.

Gwen seemed to have the monopoly on wisdom and steadiness. Every now and then, he'd glance at her over Annie's head. She kept her face forward, and the light from the screen outlined her profile. When he'd met her six years ago, he'd thought she was cute. Now she struck him as...

Beautiful. With her hair pulled back, he could see the elegant lines of her jaw and throat, the delicate hollows below her cheek bones. Her eyes were like blue topaz, clear and glittering, her lashes long and thick. Her body... She was as slender as he remembered, but more solid somehow. That body had carried his child.

He felt a sharp tug in his groin, totally inappropriate while watching a kiddie-flick with a five-year-old girl seated next to him. Totally inappropriate in any environment, he warned himself. Gwen had a lover, that guy he'd met on her front porch yesterday. Dylan was causing enough turmoil in her life without adding lust to the mix.

It had been good with her six years ago, though. Much, much better than good. What if they had another one-night-stand? Another touch-my-cheek-and-walk-away night? Could they do that without messing up Gwen's relationship with her boyfriend? Could they do it without messing up Dylan's relationship with Annie?

Was he sitting in this dark, cacophonous theater, watching a cartoon girl soar through the clouds on the back of a kite, because he wanted to be with Annie, or because he wanted to be with Gwen?

Not that Gwen particularly wanted to be with him. She was only tolerating him because he'd convinced her his disappearance from her life when she'd needed him all those years ago wasn't his fault.

It *was* his fault, of course. He'd made love with her every way he knew how that night, and then he'd walked away. She'd let him walk away. She'd seemed to feel the same way he had. She'd touched his cheek as much as he'd touched hers.

But she'd borne the consequences. He hadn't—until now.

The lights came up in the theater, startling him. One final ear-worm song blasted through the air as the credits rolled. Annie sprang from her seat and bellowed, "That was so good! Wasn't it, Mommy? Wasn't it so good?"

Gwen exchanged an amused look with Dylan over Annie's head. Her cool gray eyes seemed to communicate that she didn't think it was quite as good as Annie did, but that sitting through animated flicks about kites that sang and transported little girls through the sky was a parental duty and needed to be accepted with grace.

Gwen's knowing glance affected Dylan as much as her casual beauty did. It was a moment shared, a brief mind-meld. For that one instant, they were partners.

Then she looked down at Annie, clasped the kid's hand, and led her up the aisle, not even checking to see if Dylan was following them. He kept them in his sights as other children spilled into the aisle, bumping into him, squealing and shouting, jostling one another and tripping over the soda cups and candy wrappers littering the floor. The crowd dispersed once they entered the lobby. Dylan almost lost Gwen and Annie when he detoured to toss the empty popcorn tub in a trash can, but he spotted them near the exit and jogged past the food counter and the arcade to join them at the glass doors.

They were deep in conversation. "So you liked Maggie?" Gwen asked Annie. It took Dylan a second to remember that Maggie was the name of the movie's heroine.

Annie nodded. "She was so cool."

"What made her cool?" Gwen asked, pushing open the door. When Dylan reached behind her to hold it for them, she acknowledged him with a quick nod. At least she hadn't totally forgotten about him.

"She was very brave," Annie said. "She saved the kittens."

"I found that interesting," Gwen said, still holding Annie's hand as they crossed the parking lot to her car. "Maggie struck me as more of a dog person than a cat person."

"I'm a dog person," Annie said.

"Believe me, I know." Gwen laughed, and Dylan wondered what the joke was. "But she taught the kittens to sing."

"No," Annie corrected her. "The kite taught them to sing. She was just there."

"You're right. It was really the kite more than Maggie."

"But she was brave. The kite made her brave."

Gwen unlocked her car. Dylan had offered to drive to the theater, but Gwen had insisted on taking her car, since it had Annie's booster seat already set up in the back. He watched as she helped Annie onto the booster. Annie fastened the belt herself. Then he and Gwen climbed into the front seat and she started the engine.

Their discussion excluded him, but he appreciated the opportunity to eavesdrop. He couldn't imagine analyzing a simple children's movie so thoroughly with a five-year-old. Yet this was what parents did—good parents, anyway. They asked questions. They listened. They respected the opinions of their children. They knew how to do this.

He didn't. Sure, he talked to his nieces and his nephew, but not the way Gwen talked to Annie. Not with such deep, honest interest. He was an actor. Most of the time, when he talked to his sister's kids, he had to pretend he really cared about their soccer games and their homework assignments.

What made him think he could do this? What in the whole freaking world made him think he could be a father to Annie?

Her wildly curling hair, so much like his. That was what. Her hair and her big brown eyes, and her intensity. She was his.

He eyed Gwen, her attention on the asphalt ahead of her as she maneuvered the car through the parking lot. He couldn't hope she would ever open herself to him the way she had that one crazy night so long ago. But if he was lucky, maybe she'd teach him how to be a father.

Chapter Ten

Gwen's cell phone rang while she was driving home. She clicked the Bluetooth on her steering wheel. "Hello?"

"Gwen? It's Diana."

Gwen shot Dylan a quick look, then focused back on the road. Diana Simms was one of her good friends, even though she'd moved to Brogan's Point only last spring. She was an antiques buyer, and she'd gotten to know Gwen from selling the Attic items she'd pick up at estate sales that the auction house she worked for in Boston didn't want—downscale merchandise too new to qualify as antiques. It didn't take long for Diana and Gwen to develop a friendship. Diana's fiancé managed an assortment of programs at the community center, including the swimming lessons Annie took in the center's pool, so Gwen had known and liked him even before Diana had entered her life.

Gwen would have to tell Diana about Dylan's reappearance in her life. But she wasn't ready to talk about that yet. She wasn't even sure what there was to tell.

Unfortunately, the Bluetooth broadcast their phone conversation throughout the car. She couldn't tell Diana anything right now. "Hey, Diana. I'm on my way home," she said. "We just saw *Sky High*."

"It's a movie about a singing kite," Annie hollered from the back seat. "And kittens. And a girl."

"That's Annie," Gwen said unnecessarily. Dylan remained silent next to her. He clearly had no intention of divulging his presence, for which she was grateful.

"Are you going to get home soon? I've got a surprise for you."

"Is it a cake?" Annie asked.

"No, sugarplum," Diana's voice emerged through the dashboard speakers. "It's something for your mother's store."

Dylan twisted around to peer at Annie. Gwen saw him shrug sympathetically. The gesture touched her more than it should have.

"We'll be home in ten," she told Diana.

"I'll be over in fifteen. You're going to love this."

Gwen did a quick calculation. Did she want Diana to come over while Dylan was there? Could she get Dylan to leave as soon as they arrived at the house? Did she *want* him to leave?

Things would be easier if he did. She wouldn't have to explain him to Diana.

But he was Annie's father, and however belatedly, he wanted to fulfill his paternal obligations. He deserved a few points for trying, didn't he?

She'd withhold those points for a while. One book and one movie outing did not a father make.

Besides, she hardly knew him. One night in bed, no matter how glorious, didn't a relationship make.

She pulled into the garage and shut off the car. Behind her, she heard Annie click open her seatbelt. "I'm hungry," Annie announced. "Can we have dinner?"

"It's too early. And you just ate a ton of popcorn."

"I didn't. The man ate it all," Annie said, pointing at Dylan.

"Mr. Scott," Gwen corrected her, shooting Dylan a look. He appeared uncomfortable. Whether his discomfort was caused by being called Mr. Scott or being accused of eating all the popcorn, she didn't know.

How utterly mundane and domestic this experience must all seem to a movie star like him. How utterly boring. If he were back in Hollywood right now, he'd probably be hobnobbing with his fellow movie stars, club-hopping, jet-setting, pill-popping, whatever silver-screen celebrities did when they weren't making films. She imagined it was like some secret society out there, where all those beautiful people hung out together, drinking twenty-dollars-a-sip vodka, swapping romantic partners, and comparing their Oscar statuettes. They probably all had full-time nannies to take their children to see *Sky High* and feed them when they were hungry. Their children didn't eat mac-and-cheese out of the box. They ate lobster mac-and-cheese with truffle oil, and their chocolate milk was flavored with Godiva cocoa.

Really, what could Dylan Scott possibly want in Brogan's Point? What could he want with Gwen and Annie?

"We could go out to eat," he suggested.

"I don't think so," Gwen said as she unlocked the door and led the way into the house. For one thing, Annie had probably used up all her good behavior in the theater. She'd need to run around and let off some steam after sitting quietly for so long, and a restaurant was the last place Gwen wanted to see Annie unsteaming. For another thing, if they went out to dinner, unless they drove a few towns away, they'd undoubtedly run into someone who knew Mike. Word would get back to him that Gwen was seen dining out with Dylan. That wouldn't go over too well.

She'd have to explain the situation to Mike eventually. If Dylan intended to be a hands-on father, she'd have to let Mike know. He'd been putting some effort into bonding with Annie. How would he feel about having to compete with Dylan for the role of father?

He couldn't compete. Dylan had the biological claim.

Damn. Six years ago, she would have welcomed Dylan's participation in her life. Today, all he did was complicate the situation.

On the other hand, he could ease Annie's life financially. Gwen wouldn't have to worry about paying for Annie's college if Dylan provided child support. That seemed like an unconscionably mercenary thought, but Gwen had been a struggling single mother long enough not to care.

And then...there were other reasons to want Dylan around. Other complications. The smoky darkness of his eyes. The easy curve of his smile. His lean, lanky body. His big, strong hands. His sheer male charisma.

Her memories of that night they'd spent together. She'd never experienced anything like that before. Or since.

She felt a flush course through her body, heating her in places she didn't want to think about with a hungry daughter on the loose and a friend on her way over, and especially with the man who ignited that heat standing less than five feet away from her in her kitchen. "I'll throw something together," she said, forcing herself to focus on dinner.

Although she hadn't explicitly invited Dylan to stay, he seemed to take her words that way. "We can order take-out if you don't want to cook," he said.

"Fine." She was too distracted to cook, anyway. But she'd have to do something about Mike. She'd neglected him all weekend. Once she explained to him how Dylan was connected to her and Annie, he'd understand why she'd had to spend today with Dylan. But he probably wouldn't like it.

The doorbell rang. "That's Diana!" Annie announced, racing ahead of Gwen down the hall to the front door.

"Don't open it until I say you can," Gwen reminded Annie, scrambling to think of how she was going to explain Dylan's presence to Diana. *Oh, I just happen to be good friends with Captain Steele of the Galaxy Force. He just happened to fly his spaceship to Brogan's Point for a quick visit.* Or: *Dylan and I ran into each other at the Faulk Street Tavern and some song played and scrambled our brains.* Or: *Dylan is Annie's father.*

Swallowing, she peered through the beveled window to see Diana on the front porch, holding a large carton. "It's Diana," she told Annie, who promptly yanked the door open. "Come in," Gwen greeted her friend. "Is that heavy?"

"No, it's very light." Diana bounced into the house, preceding Gwen and Annie down the hall to the kitchen.

Annie skipped rather than walked, peppering Diana with questions about what was in the box. "Is it for me? Is it a surprise? Can I hold the box?"

"It's for your mommy's store," Diana told Annie, then froze when" she saw Dylan leaning against the counter near the sink, his hair tousled, his jacket off and slung over the back of a chair. She lowered the box to the table and gaped.

"Diana, this is Dylan Scott. Dylan, my friend Diana Simms," Gwen introduced them, then braced herself for Diana's questions.

"Captain Steele," Diana said.

"Not at the moment," Dylan responded.

"Well." Diana was usually quite chatty, but right now she seemed at a loss for words. She turned to stare at Gwen, who simply smiled and pulled a knife from the drawer to cut the carton open. She sliced through the tape and lifted the flaps. The carton was filled with cellophane-wrapped packages. Pulling one out, she laughed. The package contained two cylindrical plastic bottles with cone-shaped caps, one red and one yellow. The red one had *Squeeze Pleeze for Ketchup* printed on it, the yellow one, *Squeeze Pleeze for Mustard*.

"Where did you get these?"

"I did an estate sale this morning. The deceased had owned a chain of diners. I found three cartons of these *Squeeze Pleeze* bottles in the basement. Mint condition. Circa 1950. I can't sell them as antiques, but I'm sure you can sell them at the Attic."

"They're fabulous," Gwen said, pulling another package from the carton to make sure it contained the same ketchup and mustard containers. "Three cartons?"

"Two dozen packages per carton. Too many?"

"No, I'll take them all. How much do you want for them?"

"I was figuring seventy-five dollars for the three cartons. You can probably get ten dollars a pop for these. A very nice profit."

"Great. I love them. My customers will love them, too. They're so tacky."

"Kitsch," Diana said. "That sounds better than tacky."

Gwen laughed. "Stop by the store tomorrow. We'll do the paperwork."

"And I'll deliver the other two cartons." Her gaze strayed to Dylan. "We'll talk."

"Absolutely." Perhaps by the time she saw Diana tomorrow, Gwen would know what to say.

She walked Diana to the door, Annie trailing them, clutching a package of condiment bottles. Gwen didn't mind if the package got messed up. She'd keep that set for herself. Heaven knew if she'd ever use them, but they made her laugh, and that alone made them valuable.

Back in the kitchen, she was confronted with Dylan's presence once more. He shouldn't look so at home in such humble surroundings, but he did. Maybe it was because he was dressed not as Captain Steele but as a father who'd just taken his daughter to the movies.

Not just his daughter. He'd taken his daughter's mother to the movies, too. They'd shared the outing as a traditional domestic unit.

The idea alarmed Gwen. She mustn't think of them as a domestic unit. If Dylan wanted to build a relationship with Annie, Gwen couldn't stop him. But Annie would have to be the only link between Gwen and Dylan. His love life was much too glamorous to have room in it for someone like her.

She shouldn't even think of him in the context of a love life. She had Mike, a sales manager at Wright Honda-BMW. Dylan had gorgeous movie stars. End of story.

Still... Those eyes. That smile. Those dense brown curls. Six years ago, she'd run her fingers through those curls. She'd kissed that smile. She'd lain on top of him, below him, their bodies touching at every point, merging, fitting together like a lock and key. A dark shiver spun through her at the memory.

The wisest thing would be to ask him to leave. But the words wouldn't come.

"Can we have pizza?" Annie asked. "I love pizza."

Pizza wasn't exactly healthy—but those words wouldn't come, either. "I guess we can order a pizza," she said.

"With lots of cheese. I love cheese. What do these bottles say, Mommy? I can read 'for' but the other words are hard."

"Ask Mr. Scott," Gwen said, turning from Annie to rummage through her stack of take-out menus in the drawer beside the broom closet. If Dylan wanted to be a father, he could start by explaining phonetics to Annie.

***

The pizza was fine. The phone call from Mike wasn't. "What do you mean, I can't come over?" he asked. He didn't shout, but there was a definite rumble of anger and resentment in his voice.

"Dylan Scott is here," she told him. She didn't want to lie, but she also didn't want to go into detail with him on the phone. Was it a lie of omission that she hadn't yet told Mike that Dylan was Annie's father?

"I get it. It's a lot cooler to hang out with a movie star than with me."

"We're not hanging out," Gwen insisted. Right now, as she moved around the kitchen, flattening the empty pizza box and carrying dirty dishes to the sink, Dylan was hanging out with Annie in the basement playroom. She hoped they were reading more of the book Dylan had given Annie, but for all Gwen knew, he was teaching her how to pass a football, or how to cheat at poker, or how to handle herself on the red carpet at a film premiere. "I knew Dylan a long time ago, before he was famous," she explained carefully. "We're just catching up a little."

"How the hell did you know him? When was he not famous?"

"A long time ago," she repeated.

"So...what? I'm just supposed to sit on my hands until he leaves town? If he's an old friend of yours, he should be a friend of mine, too. If we get married, my friends will be your friends and your friends will be mine."

Not necessarily, Gwen thought. One of his closest friends was Jimmy Creighton, who worked with him at Wright Honda-BMW. Gwen had always thought Jimmy was a jerk. And Mike wasn't crazy about Gwen's friends, either—Jimmy's ex-girlfriend Monica, and Emma Glendon, who taught art classes at the community center, and Diana. Somehow, she suspected, Mike and Dylan wouldn't become pals.

But they'd have to learn to get along, if she decided to marry Mike. And if Dylan was true to his word about remaining in Annie's life.

"I don't know how long he's going to be in Brogan's Point," she told Mike. "If it's a while, of course you'll have a chance to get to know him."

"Lucky me. The big hot-shot movie star might lower himself to be friends with me."

"He's not like that." As if Gwen had any idea what Dylan was really like.

"All right," Mike said. "Tell you what. When your good friend the movie star decides he's tired of pretending he's one of us normal people, you let me know."

"Don't be that way, Mike. I've never tried to keep you from spending time with your friends."

"My friends are all guys," Mike pointed out.

True. And if Gwen was totally honest, she'd admit that her feelings for Dylan were not exactly friendly. She distrusted him. She feared the upheaval he could inflict on her life. She worried about how he'd relate to Annie, whether he'd woo the little girl with books and movies and pizza, and then walk away as he'd walked away from Gwen.

And the way he stirred a deep sexual yearning inside Gwen, a yearning she hardly recognized because it had been so long since she'd last felt it... She couldn't call that feeling "friendly," either.

"I'm sorry, Mike," she said, meaning it. "I don't know what's going on right now, but you're going to have to let me figure it out."

"Fine, babe. You figure it out. You know how to reach me when you do." With that, he disconnected the call.

Wonderful. She'd upset Mike, and she wasn't even sure what she'd upset him for. Possibly nothing, if Dylan decided fatherhood didn't interest him and he decamped for Los Angeles after a few days. Nothing, if he abandoned Annie and erased this stay in Brogan's Point from his memory. Nothing, if he walked away.

Anxiety nibbled at her gut. She'd eaten only one slice of the pizza, but she felt queasy and unsteady, as if the kitchen floor had suddenly turned to quicksand. She set down her cell phone, washed the dishes in the sink, and stacked them to dry. Then she descended the stairs to the playroom.

She found Dylan seated on the floor with Annie amid an ocean of Legos. Annie was building something and Dylan was watching her, a couple of bricks in his hands. He snapped them together, pulled them apart, then snapped them together again.

Like relationships, Gwen thought. So easy to create, so easy to break.

"It's a space ship," Annie announced, pointing to the shapeless structure she'd created. "Like what Captain Steele flies in."

Gwen eyed Dylan, who shrugged amiably. "She's the engineer. I'm just her assistant."

"I built it all myself. You know what would be really cool? If Captain Steele could fly around on a kite. He could be brave like Maggie."

"He's very brave," Gwen said, then smiled, feeling foolish. It wasn't her job to get Annie to admire Dylan. If he wanted to be her father, he would have to win her over on his own.

"He could fly into outer space on a very big, special kite," Annie explained. "With per-pellers on it, and a cat inside. He could teach the cat to sing."

"I doubt that," Dylan protested with a laugh. "I'm a terrible singer."

"But you'd be so brave, you'd sing anyway. For the cat." She added a few more bricks to her structure.

"Cat or no cat," Gwen said, "it's bath time."

"No!" Annie's face folded into a scowl. "I'm not done yet."

Gwen eyed Dylan, wondering whether he'd still want to be Annie's dad after he'd witnessed her stubbornness and her crystal-shattering whines. He met Gwen's stare, looking less alarmed than curious. Perhaps he'd dealt with temperamental little girls before. Or perhaps he was just being brave, the hero Annie wanted him to be. Little did he know that dealing with an angry, fussing little girl could require more courage than conquering extra-terrestrial villains at the far end of the galaxy.

"You can finish building the spaceship another time," Gwen said, lifting Annie's creation. "But you have to clean up all the loose Legos. We'll put the spaceship on the shelf for you to finish later."

"No! No! No!" Annie tried to pull the spaceship out of Gwen's hands. Her attempt detached a chunk of Legos and she let out a howl.

Gwen lifted what remained of the spaceship higher, out of Annie's reach, and extended her free hand to collect the other piece. "We can snap that back on," she said in a low, soothing voice. "Pick up the loose pieces, sweetie. Mr. Scott has to leave now."

Dylan shot her another look, and apparently decided not to argue. He must have realized she could handle only one defiant person at a time. With Annie battling her, she didn't want to have to battle Dylan, too, and she was grateful when he rose from the floor in a single, fluid motion and nodded at Annie. "Your mom's right," he said. "It's bath time."

"Are you going to take a bath, too?" Annie asked him, her eyes glistening with tears.

"I'm more of a shower guy, myself," he told her.

She blinked a few times, possibly to keep from crying, possibly because she didn't know how to take his comment. But she subsided before erupting into a full-blown tantrum, and occupied herself gathering the stray Lego bricks and dumping them in their bucket.

He scooped some of the Legos from the floor and added them to the bucket. His hands, so much larger than Annie's, could clean the mess more efficiently. Gwen tried to catch his eye, to signal him that it was Annie's responsibility to clean up her toys. But he'd been playing with the Legos, too, at least a little. Gwen supposed he was setting a good example by tidying up after himself.

As soon as the floor was clear, Gwen gave Annie a gentle nudge toward the stairs. "Bath time," she repeated. "Say good-bye to Mr. Scott."

"Good-bye, Mr. Scott," Annie repeated with a pout. "I don't want a bath."

"You don't want to be stinky at school tomorrow, do you?" Gwen teased, but Annie continued to sulk as she stomped up the stairs.

Gwen turned to Dylan. "It's a school night," she said, some sort of apology, although she had nothing to apologize for. He'd barged into her day and consumed nearly all of it. Letting him know she was ready for him to leave might be a bit rude, but his showing up uninvited this morning and insinuating himself into her Sunday plans had been a bit rude, too.

He seemed to realize this. "Thanks for letting me spend some time with her," he said quietly as he followed Gwen up the stairs and into the front hall. Annie had already clambered up to the bedroom level. Gwen could hear her thumping around above them. For a little girl, she could make a lot of noise. "She's great."

Yes, she is, Gwen thought, *no thanks to you.* That wasn't really fair. How could Dylan have been a father to a child he didn't know existed? Still, it had been *his* manager who'd kept him in the dark. He was the guy's boss, and he'd probably told the guy to protect him from all those crazed fans who swore they were carrying his baby.

She took a deep breath and let it out slowly. No sense getting upset about it now. The past was the past. She had to stay focused on the present and the future, on how—*if*—she and Dylan were going to be able to make this thing work.

She didn't have to shove him out the front door. He donned his leather jacket, stepped out onto the porch, and gave her an enigmatic look. Was he happy? Disappointed? Resentful?

He wasn't saying. "I'll be in touch," he told her, then pivoted and headed down the front walk to his car.

"Mommy? Can I have a bubble bath?" Annie yelled down the stairs.

Back to reality, Gwen thought, tearing her gaze from Dylan's retreating form, his broad shoulders, his sexy butt, his long, graceful stride. No time to dwell on how annoyingly attractive he was, how nice he'd been all day, how very different her life and Annie's might have been if only he'd known the truth six years ago.

Chapter Eleven

By eight-thirty, Annie was fast asleep, her outfit chosen for tomorrow and hanging from her closet door knob, her arm clutching Mr. Snuffy firmly, and her lunch box filled with a cup of yogurt, a sprig of grapes, carrot sticks, whole-wheat pretzels, and a big oatmeal cookie. She smelled like a honey-lemon drop, the scent of her bubble bath, and for all her fierce objections about having to go to bed, she'd drifted off to dreamland before Gwen had finished reading her a poem from *Now We Are Six*.

Gwen was also tired. It had been a long day. All her days were long, though: twenty-four hours packed with demands and activities and things to worry about. But she wasn't ready for bed yet. If she showered and crawled beneath the sheets, she'd only lie awake for hours, thinking about Dylan.

She hated having no control over what was happening in her life. Becoming a mother had meant ceding some control—the nerve of Annie, having a mind of her own!—but the decision to continue her pregnancy and give birth to a child had been hers alone. The decision to remain in Brogan's Point after Adam had left, and to buy out the owner of the Attic, and to purchase this house—it had all been her doing, her choice.

Dylan's plan to move to Brogan's Point was his choice, not hers. His desire to be a father to Annie was his choice. And if he decided, after a while, that he'd rather return to Hollywood and forget about the little girl he'd helped to create... Well, that would be his choice, too. Gwen wouldn't be able to prevent him from doing whatever the hell he wanted.

All she could do was try to protect Annie.

She wandered into the kitchen and poured herself a glass of chardonnay. Carrying it into the living room, she glimpsed the moon through the window overlooking her front yard. It was a sharp crescent, a silver smile tilted sideways in the starlit autumn sky. The street was quiet, the night tranquil. Five years after Annie's birth, Gwen continued to be amazed at how peaceful the world seemed when her daughter was asleep.

She pulled her barn jacket from the coat closet, slipped it on, and stepped out onto the front porch, wine glass in hand. The night was cool but not cold, the air crisp with the tart scent of apples and pine. Lowering herself to sit on the porch steps, she gazed upward, picking out the Big and Little Dippers, the three stars of Orion's belt, the bright white dot of Venus.

Sitting beneath the vast night sky, Gwen felt her worries settle inside her, growing still. Everything would work out somehow. She'd figure things out with Mike. She'd let Annie get to know Dylan—that would have probably happened in some form, sooner or later—and she'd be the best mother she knew how to be. At least that was something she could control.

She took a sip of the cold, dry wine, then sighed. Then spotted the car parked across the street from her, the door opening, the man emerging. The dome light inside the vehicle illuminated his face, but she would have recognized him by nothing more than the faint light of the moon catching in the dense curls of his hair.

Had Dylan remained seated in his car in front of the Nolan house while Gwen had been monitoring Annie's bath time and packing her lunch box? Or had he driven somewhere for the past hour and a half, and then come back?

She'd have the chance to ask him, because he closed the car door and ambled across the street and up her front walk. He offered a hesitant smile as he joined her on the porch, lowering himself to sit beside her.

"Have you been parked in front of my neighbor's house all this time?" were the first words out of her mouth.

He shrugged, then nodded. "I've been busy. My manager sent me a bunch of stuff to read. Contracts for a Galaxy Force computer game and app."

"You could have gone back to...wherever it is you're staying to do your reading."

"I could have." He rested his forearms on his knees and stared out into the dark. "It's a nice night."

"That's not why you sat reading contracts in your car."

"No." He shot a fleeting look her way. "I wanted to talk to you. I feel like there's so much we have to talk about, and I don't even know where to start."

That he was willing to reveal his confusion touched her. Dylan Scott—the successful hot-shot movie star—looked lost and vulnerable, his expression an intriguing blend of hope and fear. "You could start by telling me if you thought Maggie was brave," she joked, trying to put him at ease.

He chuckled, then grew solemn. "The way you talked to Annie about the movie—I wouldn't know how to do that. I've got nieces and a nephew, but—I mean, how to you know what to ask? How to you draw her ideas out of her?"

"She's my daughter," Gwen said. She'd never really had to contemplate how to engage Annie in a conversation. She'd been talking to Annie from the moment Annie had been born, when the midwife had swaddled her in a soft cotton blanket and handed her into Gwen's eager arms.

Before then, actually. Gwen used to whisper to her swollen abdomen when she was pregnant, promising the tiny life inside her that she loved it and would take care of it, no matter what.

"I need to learn so much." Dylan sighed. "I feel completely ignorant."

"Not ignorant. Inexperienced," Gwen told him. "You'll learn." She realized she'd just conceded that Dylan would be a fixture in Annie's life. How else would he gain experience, if not by talking to Annie as often as possible, the way Gwen did?

He sent her another look, his expression dubious and tinged with panic. She handed him her glass of wine. He smiled and took a sip. "Liquid courage," he joked. "Why did you name her Annie?"

"You don't like the name?"

"It's a great name. I'm just curious why you chose it."

"It's my grandmother's name. Gwendolyn was my mother's grandmother's name. That's how we do things in my family."

He nodded. "Better than my family. I was named after Bob Dylan. My sisters are Janis—as in Janis Joplin—and Grace—as in Grace Slick. My parents loved Sixties rock music."

"I guess you're lucky they didn't name you Elvis," she teased.

He handed back her wine glass. It occurred to her that sharing her wine with him was an intimate thing to do. As was sharing her porch step, which was small enough that there were only a few inches of air between his shoulder and hers. His smell mixed with the smells of autumn, a warm, male scent. When they talked like this, seated on the hard concrete of a suburban porch, he didn't seem like a famous actor at all. He seemed just like...a man.

"You never considered getting an abortion?" he asked. "I mean, after you realized I wasn't going to step up."

"I thought about it." She lapsed into silence, remembering those dark days when Dylan's manager had threatened to bring charges against her if she attempted to reach him again. By then, she'd been closing in on her twelfth week of pregnancy, and she hadn't had time to linger over the decision. So she'd sat down and written a list of pros and cons.

Raising a child herself, far from her parents. Running the store as a single parent. Dealing with the repercussions once her child learned that she was the daughter of a famous actor, because by then, Dylan

Scott was famous. Financial concerns. Social concerns. The cons list
had been pretty long.

The pros list had been short: *I want this baby.* Period. And that had
decided her.

"It was your choice to make," Dylan said, shifting so he could look
at her. "I'm glad you chose to keep her. I wouldn't have blamed you if
you hadn't, but I'm glad you did."

"I've never had a moment's regret," she told him.

He continued to gaze at her. The dim moonlight drained the color
from him; his face was an arrangement of angles and shadows, his eyes
as dark as the sky above them. He eased her wine glass from her hand,
and she expected him to take another sip. But he only placed it on the
porch, then slid his hand under her hair until his palm covered her
cheek, warming it. He dipped his face to hers.

She shouldn't do this. But they were sharing wine, and the porch,
and the starlit sky. They were sharing a daughter.

When his lips touched hers, she sighed.

In her memory, the night they'd spent together so long ago had
been a rowdy, energetic affair. He'd been exhilarated by the completion
of his work in *Sea Glass*, and she'd been rejuvenated by the
comprehension that this cool, gorgeous guy found her attractive, that
she could think of herself not as the victim of a painful break-up, not as
a cast-off ex, but as a healthy, physical woman who could enjoy sex.

Just as she'd had no regrets about continuing her pregnancy, she'd
had no regrets about her night of love-making with Dylan.

If that had been an exuberant celebration, this kiss was nothing
of the sort. It was quiet, tender, questioning. Without words, he was
asking her if kissing her was allowed, if it was acceptable.

For heaven's sake—he'd seen her naked. He'd kissed and licked and
nipped every square inch of her body. She couldn't very well insist she
was a modest, proper lady now.

Besides, his mouth felt good on hers. Warm. Sweet. His kiss stirred a longing deep inside her, a need she'd suppressed ever since...

Ever since his manager had slammed the door on her. That virtual slam had obliterated the woman who enjoyed sex, who had embraced Dylan as eagerly as he'd embraced her, who had acknowledged her needs and wants and desires. From that moment on, she'd viewed herself as someone Dylan wanted to forget, a bit-part actor in a scene left on the cutting room floor. She'd edited out a part of herself, too—the carefree, reckless, sensuous part—and cast herself in the role of a responsible mother.

Now she was more. She was a woman, reveling in the sensations Dylan aroused within her.

His hand remained warm against her cheek, his fingers twirling gently through her hair. She lifted her hands to his shoulders, and he tilted his head slightly, deepening the kiss. His tongue slid along the seal of her lips, and she parted them to allow him in. A soft groan escaped him.

Oh, God, this felt good. It felt luscious. It felt right.

But as unexpectedly as the kiss began, he ended it, leaning back, twisting away, tilting his head until he was staring straight up at the sky. "Sorry," he said.

Really? He was sorry?

"I shouldn't—I mean, I've already messed your life up in more ways than I can count," he said, addressing the moon as much as Gwen. "You've got a life here, you've got a boyfriend... It's just..."

He might be an actor, but he didn't have any rehearsed lines. His struggle to articulate his thoughts touched her almost as much as his kiss had.

"I had a good time today. With you and Annie. But—I mean, let's face it. It was damned presumptuous of me, just sweeping in, imposing myself on you like this."

Did he want to leave? Not just her porch but her world—did he want to back out, return to Hollywood, run away?

"I just barged in, uninvited. Ta-*dah*, here I am, let me in. Drinking your wine, building spaceships with your daughter. Yeah, presumptuous. And ..." He gestured vaguely toward her face, then traced her lower lip with his thumb before turning away. "*That*. I don't know what I was thinking."

Whatever he'd been thinking when they kissed, now he was probably thinking he wanted out. This entire day had been way too domestic for him, way too un-Hollywood.

If that was his choice, Gwen wouldn't stop him. She and Annie had survived without him all these years. They could survive without him again, if they had to.

Yet the thought of Dylan's vanishing upset her more now than it had six years ago. Then, she'd been prepared for him to vanish. It had been understood, part of the deal. They'd never spent a day together, gone to a movie together, eaten pizza together. They'd never been an actual family together.

Today, they *had* been a family, at least for a few hours. It had felt that way to her, anyway.

Probably not to him. Today might have been nothing more than a performance to him. He'd take his curtain calls—did movie stars do that? Did they bow and bask in the applause?—and he'd hop on the next plane back to Los Angeles, and Gwen and Annie would be on their own.

Maybe, if she asked, he'd help out with some child support payments every now and then. In the meantime, though, she'd have to forget how lovely his kiss had been. How appealing she'd found his smile. How ridiculously attractive he was.

She could do that. She was old enough to face the dawn.

Where had that thought come from? A melody echoed faintly inside her skull. *Just call me angel of the morning...* That song from the jukebox at the Faulk Street Tavern. A song about letting someone go. Kissing him, making love with him, and then watching him turn away.

"It's getting cold," she said, shrugging her jacket more snugly around herself. "And late. I should go in."

Dylan looked rueful. When she stood, he hoisted himself to his feet as well. "Gwen—"

"No, really. I'm going in. Good night, Dylan." Abrupt, yes. But she'd be damned if she'd watch him turn away. *She* was the one who was going to turn away. Let him be the one who watched.

Chapter Twelve

"They accepted your bid," Andrea Simonetti said.

Dylan rubbed his chin, hoping the friction of his thumb against his overnight stubble of beard would somehow spark his brain into gear. This was good news. He ought to be happy. He *was* happy. Better than happy. If the owner of that sprawling house overlooking the ocean had agreed to Dylan's price, he could buy the place. He could live in Brogan's Point. Near his daughter.

Near Gwen.

Andrea's good news didn't jolt him to life the way it should, though. He hadn't slept much last night, and he was feeling bleary. Cell phone pressed to his ear, he shoved back the blankets and padded across the room to the courtesy coffee pot sitting on a tray on the dresser. With his free hand and his teeth, he managed to tear open the envelope containing the coffee. He tamped it into the coffee maker's basket, then filled the pot with water in the bathroom and poured it into the well.

"Are you there, Dylan?"

"Yeah, I'm here. Rough night," he said laconically. Not the sort of rough night usually associated with Hollywood types. No intoxicants had been involved, no glamorous women, no giddy groupies. Just a long, dark stretch of hours filled with thoughts of Gwen. Thoughts he shouldn't be having.

The room was chilly, and all he had on was a pair of boxer briefs. If the house sale went through and he relocated to Brogan's Point, he was going to have to get used to chilly air, cold floorboards against his bare feet, clanking radiators, and raw, misting rain like the damp morning outside his window.

He could handle all kinds of weather. He'd grown up in Nebraska, after all, where rain was always welcome because his grandparents' farm needed it, and because at least it wasn't snow.

Still, while his coffee brewed, there was no reason he couldn't crawl back under the blankets, into the warm nest of the bed. "So what happens now?" he asked Andrea, pulling the blanket up over his body and letting his head sink into the plush down pillows.

"You come into my office and we draw up a binder. You'll need to write a check, one percent of the sales price should be fine. That will be held in escrow—"

"Right. I know. I've bought a house before." He'd gone through the same basic process when purchasing his home in Venice Beach. He'd sold that house a month ago for a nice profit. Most of his possessions were currently stashed in a storage unit, and he'd been camping out in Barry Hoffman's guest house while preparing for his trip east. Barry was Dylan's lawyer and his friend. As an attorney to movie stars, he made more money than most of his clients did. He owned a sprawling estate in Brentwood, and he'd generously made his guest house available until Dylan figured out where he was going to live.

In Brogan's Point. He was going to live here, in that house overlooking the Atlantic Ocean. Just a few miles from his daughter.

A few miles from Gwen.

Suddenly he felt warmer. He kicked back the covers and smiled. When he'd arrived in Brogan's Point a few days ago, he'd been leaving something: all the shit he had to put up with in Hollywood, the type-casting, the rejection, the frustration of wanting to grow professionally, to tackle new challenges, to be viewed as more than a cartoonish superhero. He'd never imagined this move would turn out to be not about leaving something but about coming to something: a daughter. A woman who'd lit him up like a Roman candle one glorious, explosive night six years ago. A woman he'd kissed last night and wanted in a crazy way this morning.

Sure, she had a boyfriend. Yeah, he'd barged into her life and messed it up. So what? He was Captain Steele. He was one of the good guys. He could make this right.

"Get the paperwork started," he told Andrea. "I'll bring my checkbook."

***

He stopped in at the Attic after spending an hour with Andrea at her real estate office, reviewing the sales agreement, signing papers, and writing a big, fat check. The house wasn't his yet. It had to undergo inspection, a deed search, a tax appraisal, and assorted other bureaucratic things. Still, Dylan could scarcely contain his euphoria when he bounded into the Attic a little before noon in search of Gwen.

As soon as he stepped inside the store, he spotted her ringing up a purchase at the counter near the entrance. She flicked a glance his way and her lips tightened slightly. He refused to let her obvious apprehension spoil his mood. Instead, he unzipped his jacket and waited patiently while she and the customer chatted about some issue concerning the cod population off Cape Ann. If Dylan made Brogan's Point his home, he supposed he'd have to pay attention to issues like the cod population, too. This was a fishing town. He figured he could learn to discuss cod knowledgeably, the way he used to be able to discuss corn-based ethanol while he was growing up in Nebraska.

Gwen's eyes were stunning, he realized as he observed her and the customer conversing. She wore no make-up, which somehow made her gaze appear more focused, more intense. Even from a distance, he could see the vivid silver-gray of her irises, the delicate strands of her lashes. Her hands moved constantly as she spoke, inserting the woman's credit card in the chip scanner, wrapping her purchase in tissue paper and sliding it into a bag imprinted with "The Attic" and the image of a peaked roof, or simply fluttering in the air, her fingers dancing as she described something. He recalled the way her hands had felt on his body all those years ago. Amazing how keen that memory was.

Of course, that long-ago memory had been revived by last night's kiss. Which had been a mistake, a breach of boundaries, but he didn't care. He wanted her.

Finally, the woman took her bag and departed, and Dylan hustled over to the counter. "Good morning," he said, hoping to thaw her with a smile his manager assured him could melt female hearts from a mile away.

Maybe it wasn't so effective close up. Gwen's gorgeous eyes narrowed and her graceful hands got busy buttoning her sweater, as if she needed extra protection from him. "It's almost afternoon," she pointed out.

"Then it must be lunchtime. Can I take you to lunch? I drove past a diner this morning. Bailey's, I think."

"Riley's," she corrected him. "I can't leave the store. The lunch hour is a busy time for us."

"You've got other clerks," he said, pointing to two women standing in front of a framed oval full-length mirror, one draping a shawl over the other's shoulders.

"I'm sorry," Gwen said, the ice in her tone melting the slightest bit. "I really can't leave for lunch."

"Maybe I could bring something in for you," he offered. "There's that cookie store down the street."

She rolled her eyes and laughed. "Cookie's. It's going to be my downfall. I gain ten pounds every time I enter that store."

He eyed her up and down. She didn't look ten pounds too heavy. She looked perfect. "It's just that I've got some news I need to share with you, and I don't want to do it on the fly. Are you free for dinner?"

"No."

Her abrupt answer caused a picture to flash across his mind—not Annie, but that guy. Her boyfriend. What the hell was his name?

Shit. Dylan wasn't a poacher. He didn't make a habit of cutting in on couples who were dancing happily. If Gwen and her boyfriend had a good thing going, Dylan was going to have to back off.

But he was Annie's father. No matter if Gwen wanted to stay with the boyfriend, marry him, pop out a few more adorable children with him—Annie was still Dylan's daughter. Nothing Gwen did would change that.

He'd learn how to talk to Annie. He'd learn how to ask her about animated movie characters. He'd build spaceships out of Legos with her. He'd bring her to the set when he started filming the next Galaxy Force movie, and introduce her to the other actors, and he'd show her how the CGI wizards created the special effects that made it look as if Dylan was wrestling with a six-armed alien when, in fact, he was simply performing a choreographed solo in front of a green screen.

He would be the coolest daddy in the world. Gwen could have her boyfriend. Dylan would win the heart of at least one Parker female.

He gazed at Gwen across the counter. Her mouth was set in a prim line, her complexion creamy, her brow smooth. But her eyes looked troubled, turbulent. "You kissed me back," he reminded her. "Last night. It wasn't a one-sided thing."

"It should never have happened," she argued, her voice hushed, her gaze darting around the store to see if anyone was eavesdropping. "I hardly know you."

He almost laughed. She'd hardly known him six years ago, and she'd gleefully redefined X-rated with him.

But she hadn't been a mother then.

And she hadn't had a boyfriend, at least as far as Dylan knew.

"All right." He sighed, forcing contrition into his tone. "I overstepped last night. I'm sorry. I like you, Gwen. Maybe we hardly know each other, but that can change."

"It can't change right now," she said, peering past him and nodding. He turned to see the customer with the shawl approaching the counter.

She was doing everything in her power to push him away. Ordinarily, he'd respect that. But he was the father of her daughter. They were family.

Dylan had learned a long time ago not to let rejection discourage him. If he could be defeated that easily, he would never have become Captain Steele. You couldn't succeed in show business if you accepted no for an answer every time.

Besides... *She'd kissed him.* She'd been into it as much as he had, at least for a magic moment.

"Okay. Look. Tell me when you can fit me in," he said, even as Gwen smiled at the customer and folded the shawl neatly. "It's really important."

She held up her index finger, which he took to mean he should wait, and then immersed herself in a conversation with the customer, complimenting her on her taste in choosing the shawl, discussing retro styles, agreeing that the garment would look really cool with a long-sleeved T-shirt, skinny jeans, and boots. Dylan pictured Gwen in just such a get-up. He pictured himself easing the shawl off her shoulders, then sliding his hands under the shirt...

He shook off the image and waited, thinking someone ought to point out to Gwen that engaging every customer in a lengthy chat at the check-out counter was hardly efficient. Yet her customers seemed to appreciate her friendliness. Hell, what did he know about retail? Gwen was probably winning their loyalty for life, simply by being herself.

A few more customers entered as he stood idly beside a shelf of snow globes. He wondered where she would display the ketchup and mustard sets her friend had brought her yesterday. There seemed to be no underlying theme to what she sold, other than that everything might be found in someone's cluttered attic. Maybe that was all the theme she needed.

He watched the customers wander deeper into the store—the start of the noontime rush, perhaps—and hoped they wouldn't race to the counter with their purchases before he had a chance to speak once more with Gwen. He wasn't sure why she was slamming the door on him, other than her boyfriend situation. And his forwardness last night. And possibly the fact that, as far as she knew, he was merely passing through town. He had to cross that notion off her list and tell her about the house purchase. But not in a rush, between customers.

At last the shawl purchaser departed. He stepped to the counter. "It's important," he repeated. "Let me give you my private number." Before she could argue, he plucked a pen from a decorative cup beside the register, and one of the store bags. He jotted his cell number on the bag and nudged it across the counter to her. "I'm trusting you not to pass that along to anyone else," he said. "Call me when you have a minute. It's *really* important."

She took the bag, folded it, slid it beneath the counter. Someplace safe, he hoped. Her eyes remained on him, glimmering with questions and confusion, misgivings and yearning. At least he hoped it was yearning he was seeing in those cool silver depths. It definitely wasn't hatred.

He smiled, resisted the urge to lean over the counter and touch his lips to hers, and strode out of the store.

Chapter Thirteen

After Dylan left, Gwen cut out the section of the shopping bag on which he had printed his number, using the scissors she kept behind the counter. She tossed the rest of the bag into the trash and tucked his number into her pocket. She wasn't sure she was ready to enter it in her phone.

She would have to eventually, of course. Whether or not he walked away this time, he knew about Annie now, and Gwen might have to contact him—for child support, or to ask about his medical history, or something.

As if the only subject she'd ever want to contact him about was Annie.

She'd made a plan with Mike to meet for dinner tonight. He'd phoned her that morning, apologized for their telephone spat yesterday, and asked her to find a sitter. He had suggested that she come to his house for dinner, but that seemed risky to her. She wasn't sure yet what she was going to say to him, but whatever it was, she'd rather say it in a public place. And if she went to his apartment, he might expect her to jump into bed with him. They hadn't made love in days. She wished she'd missed having sex with him, but she didn't.

As anxious as she felt about what was going on in her life, and as contrite as she felt about the impact it would have on Mike, she wasn't going to go to bed with him just to smooth things out between them, to make him feel better or atone for the sins she felt accumulating in her soul. She had plenty to atone for: Not having told him who Annie's father was right from the start. Not having told him after he'd met Dylan on her front porch. Not making love with him. Not minding that they hadn't made love.

Kissing Dylan. Thinking about him all night. Thinking about kissing him again. Thinking about what making love with him had been like all those years ago. Missing *that*. Wishing she could relive that long-ago night, experience that steamy splendor one more time before she settled for Mike.

Realizing that if she married Mike, she would be settling.

At one time, settling had seemed like her most reasonable option. Her daughter needed a father. Gwen wanted stability in her life, and a partner by her side to help her face the inevitable challenges and crises that loomed in her future, and in Annie's. Mike was a decent guy. He had his faults—who didn't?—but he'd accepted Gwen. Most men, she'd learned, wanted nothing to do with a woman whose life revolved around a demanding young daughter.

She had no idea what Dylan wanted. She knew, though, that he wasn't like most men.

She had told Mike she would meet him at the Lobster Shack at six-thirty. They would be able to feast on fresh seafood there, at cheap prices. She would treat. It was the least she could do.

The afternoon passed in a blur. A satisfying number of customers entered the Attic. Most of them bought something. Gwen chatted with every patron, and no one she talked to could have guessed how distracted she was. Schmoozing with customers was one of the things she did well, and one of the main reasons the Attic remained profitable.

At around three, Diana Simms dropped by to deliver the cartons of Squeeze-Pleeze ketchup and mustard bottles. Gwen ushered her to the office in back so she could write up a purchase order and cut a check. As soon as they were shut inside the room, Diana sprang like a hungry leopard on its prey. "Tell me all about Dylan Scott," she demanded, her eyes bright with curiosity. "How could you not tell me you were friends with Captain Steele?"

"We're not friends, exactly," Gwen hedged as she helped Diana stack the cartons atop Annie's coloring table in one corner of the room. She was glad to have the boxes to focus on. If she looked directly at Diana, Diana would surely be able to read in her face that there was a hell of a lot more going on than friendship, or *not*-friendship, between Gwen and Dylan. "We knew each other a long time ago."

"How? Do you have a show-biz history I know nothing about?"

"He was here in Brogan's Point making a movie. This was years ago, before he was famous. It was a little low-budget film called *Sea Glass*. Nothing like the Galaxy Force movies."

"And you got to know him? Gwen!" Diana poked Gwen in the shoulder. "That's so exciting! Does he invite you to movie premieres? Could you be his date for the Oscars?"

"Oh, please." Gwen forced a laugh. "When he was here making *Sea Glass*, the movie's art director bought some stuff at the Attic, and Dylan came with her. We talked a few times. That's all."

"That's not all. An A-list movie star doesn't just turn up in your kitchen because you talked to him a few times before he was famous."

"He was passing through town. We ran into each other. I invited him back for pizza."

"Well, isn't that special." Gwen could hear the sarcasm in her friend's voice. Reluctantly, she turned to face Diana, who stood near the desk, her hands on her hips and her brow creased in a frown. "Tell me the truth, or you can't be a bridesmaid," she threatened. Her wedding to Nick Fiore, who coordinated youth programs at the community center, was just a couple of months away.

Gwen refused to take the threat seriously. She laughed, and Diana joined her. "The truth? Dylan is Annie's father."

Diana stopped laughing. Her eyes nearly popped out of their sockets. "You're kidding."

"No. And please don't tell anyone."

"Sworn to secrecy." Diana traced an X on her chest with her finger, crossing her heart. "You slept with him? Really?"

"Really. One night of craziness. These things happen."

"Not with gorgeous movie stars."

"Especially with them," Gwen said.

Diana conceded with a smile and a nod. "So...he was in your kitchen to visit his daughter?"

"He didn't even know he had a daughter until just now," Gwen explained. "When I found out I was pregnant, I tried to reach him, but his manager ran interference and I was never able to get through to him. Now he knows, and he wants to be a part of her life." She sighed. "It's messy."

"Do you want him in her life?"

"Well... He's her father." And if he was in Annie's life, he'd be in Gwen's life, too. But not in her life the way she wanted a man to be in her life. He *was* a movie star, after all. He'd be jetting to locations and reported on in gossip magazines and on show-biz websites. He'd be photographed at the Oscars with gorgeous young women, not with Gwen.

She recalled all the reasons she'd considered accepting Mike's proposal. Dylan promised none of them. No stability. No reliable presence in Annie's life. No partner to stand by Gwen and help her face whatever life threw at her.

"I've got to run," Diana said, accepting the check and receipt Gwen handed her. "I still have a ton of pieces to inventory from the estate sale. It wasn't all condiment bottles. The guy liked kitsch, but he also had some remarkable items. His granddaughter gave me some paperwork claiming a sculpture he had was a genuine Henry Moore, but I need to set up an appraisal." She gave Gwen a quick hug. "If you want to bring Captain Steele to the wedding as your plus-one, let me know before we lock in the catering order."

Gwen laughed away her offer. The way things were going, Mike might not be her plus-one, either. Maybe she'd bring Annie along as her date.

***

At five o'clock, she left the store in the capable hands of her assistant manager and raced off to pick up Annie at her after-school program. The rain had ebbed into a light, raw mist, and her car's headlights glared against the wet roadways. She tried to plan what she would say to Mike, but her brain was too muddled. The only thing she could focus on was getting to the after-school program before five-fifteen. If she showed up late, she would get charged a penalty.

She made it to the parking lot with a minute to spare. Annie greeted her with a hug and a monologue about the paper skeleton she and the other students were constructing. "We used oak tag for the bones, and butterfly clips, so their joints move. My bones don't look so good, but the teacher said they were fine. The skull is really important. I'll work on that tomorrow. It's for Halloween," she added unnecessarily. "We can hang it on the door. When are we going to buy a pumpkin, Mommy? Can we make a jackie-lantern?"

"Maybe we'll go to the farm stand this weekend," Gwen offered.

"Can I pick my own pumpkin? I want a really big one."

"It has to be small enough for you to carry," Gwen warned her. Left to her own devices, Annie would choose a pumpkin twice her own size.

"Can I cut the jackie-lantern?"

"No. You can draw the face, and I'll do the cutting."

"I'm big enough. I won't cut myself."

"I'll do the cutting," Gwen repeated in a firm tone. She knew Annie would pester her again in a couple of days about carving her own jack-o-lantern—and maybe in a couple of days, Gwen would have the strength to explain to her once more why she was too young to hack through the pumpkin's tough exterior with a sharp knife. But now, she just wanted the debate to end.

"What are we having for dinner?"

"I'm meeting Mike for dinner tonight," Gwen told Annie. "I'm sorry, but we need to discuss some grown-up things. Hayley from down the street is going to babysit for you."

"I like Hayley," Annie said. "She's so pretty. And she lets me have ice-cream."

Gwen wasn't going to lecture Annie—or, for that matter, Hayley—on nutrition. If the kid wanted ice-cream tonight, she could have ice-cream.

She made quick work of cleaning out Annie's lunch box and cooking a turkey burger and steamed carrots for her. Hayley showed up at a quarter past six, and Gwen bolted for the Lobster Shack, still dressed in the sweater set and slacks she'd worn all day at work. As she settled into the driver's seat, she felt something crinkling in her pocket. She slid her hand in and felt the scrap of paper with Dylan's phone number on it.

She still had no idea just what she would say to Mike. All she knew, as dread tightened its hold on her, was that it wouldn't go well.

She arrived at the wharf-side restaurant before he did. In addition to its tasty food and low prices, the Lobster Shack was blessed with having not one scintilla of romantic atmosphere. The walls were rough-hewn plank paneling, the tables were topped with paper placemats, and the only nautical decoration was a clock shaped like a ship's steering wheel hanging on one wall. Less than a minute after Gwen told the hostess she was waiting for her companion, Mike walked in.

He looked good. He always did. He was a handsome guy, with a broad, square face and reddish-brown hair that was beginning to thin, although still plentiful enough that his comb-over camouflaged the thin spots. He had taken the time to change into a flannel shirt and jeans, not what he wore when he was selling Hondas at Wright Honda-BMW. But then, he hadn't had to pick up a daughter and feed her dinner before coming to the Lobster Shack.

The waitress seated them. Mike ordered fish and chips and a beer, Gwen a lobster roll and water. No wine. She needed her wits about her. Besides, the wines at the Lobster Shack were pretty bad: generic red, generic white, generic rose, which she suspected might just be equal parts of the red and white mixed together.

While they waited for their food, Mike shared with her a convoluted anecdote having to do with floor mats and cup holders in a car he'd recently sold. Gwen did her best to nod and look interested. She tried to guess whether Mike's decision to avoid mentioning their argument yesterday was a good or a bad thing.

Finally their meals arrived. Gwen gazed down at the submarine roll sliced lengthwise and overflowing with shiny red and white chunks of lobster meat. The Lobster Shack made the best lobster rolls south of Maine, but she had no appetite.

"I have to tell you something, Mike," she said, picking at the lobster meat with her fork.

He shrugged and took a hefty swig of beer. "I'm all ears."

"Dylan Scott? The actor you saw at my house Saturday?"

Mike nodded.

"He's Annie's father. She doesn't know that yet, and I'd appreciate it if you didn't tell her. I'll tell her when I think the time is right. But it has to be done properly."

"He's her father?" Mike bellowed.

"Shh."

Mike scanned the room, but none of the other diners seemed particularly aware of his outburst. "He's her father?" he said more quietly. "Her effing *father*?"

"Yes."

Mike chewed on a French fry, and simultaneously ruminated on this news. "Some hell of a father he is. Where has he been all of Annie's life?"

"He didn't know about her. There was...a communications breakdown."

"Oh. A communications breakdown." Mike's gaze narrowed on Gwen, but he didn't stop eating. "So, how did that happen? How did you wind up having a kid with a movie star? You were—what? Some groupie or something? Do movie stars have groupies? I thought that was just rock stars."

"I wasn't a groupie. It was..." She sighed. She honestly didn't want to explain to Mike her history with Dylan. It had been hard enough explaining it to Diana, and Diana was her friend. And a woman. Mike was a guy. "He wasn't a movie star when we..."

"When you screwed. When you made a baby. She's, what, six years old? He wasn't a movie star then?"

"She's five. I knew him six years ago. And no, he wasn't a movie star then. He was a struggling actor."

Mike ate for a while in silence, his jaw moving slowly, his eyes narrowed on her. How could she possibly eat when he was staring at her that way, so full of anger and resentment?

"I'm sorry," she said. "It was a shock to me, too, his showing up in town unexpectedly. And he saw Annie, and..." She detected no softening in Mike's expression. "I'm sorry," she said quietly.

He crumpled his napkin into a ball, slugged down the rest of his beer, and stood. "I have to think," he muttered. "This is too much." With that, he stalked out of the restaurant.

Gwen had planned to pay for their meal, but Mike's abrupt departure, before she could even make the offer, irked her. She gazed at her lobster roll for a long, helpless minute, then signaled the waitress and asked her to wrap it to go. Once she'd settled the bill, she left the Lobster Shack.

The air was cool and damp, heavy with the salty scent of the ocean. The wharf's planks were damp, too, and slightly slippery. She picked way carefully to the asphalt of the parking lot, climbed into her car, and tossed her sandwich onto the passenger seat. Then she reached into her pocket and pulled out the paper with Dylan's phone number on it.

Chapter Fourteen

He was in his hotel room, nursing a glass of scotch, when his cell phone rang. His room service dinner sat untouched under an aluminum lid. He couldn't even remember what he'd ordered.

He'd been waiting all afternoon for the familiar chime of his phone, but the only time it had rung, the caller had been Andrea, informing him that she'd set up an appointment for a walk-through of the house with an inspector.

Fine. Great. The house would get inspected.

Had he been too pushy with Gwen? Too presumptuous? Did she not want him in Annie's life? How could they possibly coexist in Brogan's Point if Gwen intended to keep him from his daughter?

And from herself?

Shit. If he'd gotten the part in *The Angel*, he might have stayed in Los Angeles. If he hadn't come to Brogan's Point, he never would have known about Annie. If he hadn't seen the house for sale, if he hadn't made a bid on it, if he hadn't walked into the Faulk Street Tavern and heard that song play, and seen Gwen... If, if, if.

But his phone was ringing now, too late for Andrea to be announcing some other important development in the bureaucratic process of purchasing a house. He set down his glass, reached for the phone, and glanced at the screen. No name, just a number. "Hello," he said.

"Dylan? It's Gwen."

His day got marginally brighter—even though the sun had set long ago and the moon was obliterated by clouds and mist. "Hi," he said, trying not to sound too excited.

"You said you wanted to talk," she reminded him.

"In person." Maybe he was being presumptuous again, but screw it. He wanted to see her. He wanted to see her face when he told her he'd signed a contract to buy a house in Brogan's Point. He wanted to gauge her reaction. He wanted to figure out a way to make this work. "Can I come over?"

"I'm not home," she told him. He recalled her saying she wasn't available for dinner that night. Was she on a date right now, phoning him in front of her boyfriend? That would be pretty rude.

"Then come here. I'm at the Ocean Bluff Inn."

She laughed, although she didn't sound amused. "I'm not coming to your room."

He remembered what had happened the last time she'd come to his hotel room. God, he'd like to have that happen again. But clearly it wasn't going to happen tonight. "How about the Faulk Street Tavern? Will you meet me there?"

"Okay. I'll be there in ten minutes."

"I'll see you." Just saying those three words made his day brighten even more—brighten enough for him to believe the sun was glaring through the window, burning right through the walls, even though it was well past seven o'clock.

He was going to see Gwen. He was going to tell her. *Please, make this be okay.*

***

Monday was usually a pretty slow night at the tavern—which meant the place was about half full when Gus spotted the movie guy entering. He was alone, just as he'd been a couple of days ago, and she waited for him to cross the room and plant himself on one of the empty stools at the bar. Margie Carerra looked as if she hoped the stool he'd plant himself on was the one next to hers. She had a few years on him, but she was pretty enough, and she stayed in good shape. She nearly always came to the tavern alone. It was her habit to nurse a Cosmo and survey the room, scouting for prospects.

She definitely perked up when the movie guy walked in. "Am I crazy, or is that Dylan Scott?" she murmured to Gus.

Gus shot a glance his way before resuming the task of refilling a row of bowls with bar snacks. He looked scruffy, just as he had the other day, not like a clean-cut, well-scrubbed, All-American hero prepared to conquer alien foes throughout the universe. Like the last time he'd been in, he wore a pair of comfortably broken-in jeans and a rumpled leather jacket. His hair was a lush mop of brown that glistened from the raindrops trapped in the waves.

"That's him," Gus confirmed. "But don't get your hopes up. Last time he was here, I think the jukebox got him."

Margie sighed. "Why doesn't that damned jukebox ever work for me?" she asked. "I could use some magic in my life."

Gus shrugged. "Sometimes a person has to make her own magic."

"I wouldn't mind making magic with him." Margie motioned toward the actor with her chin.

"Keep coming," Gus told her. "Keep sticking quarters into the jukebox. One of these days..." She shrugged. "You never know." She didn't bother to add that a song from the jukebox wasn't necessary for a person to find true love. Look at her and Ed Nolan. They'd just sort of stumbled onto each other, a middle-aged widow who owned a bar and a middle-aged widower who dealt with his grief by visiting that bar a bit too often. The irony was that Gus, who owned the bar, had to convince Ed to cut down on his drinking. Not good for business, but good for his health, and his soul.

The entrance door swung open, but Gus held out no hope that the new arrival was Ed. He'd phoned her earlier to tell her he was having dinner with his daughter, Maeve. Ever since Maeve had returned to town a month ago, she and Ed had been rebuilding their relationship, one brick at a time. Or maybe one cookie at a time. Maeve had opened that cookie bakery on Seaview Avenue. The girl could win anyone's heart with her cookies—although she seemed to have won the only heart she cared about. From what Ed had told Gus, and what Gus could see for herself, Quinn Connor was totally smitten with Maeve. Who would have thought the hot-shot high school hero and the shy baker would hit it off?

They'd gotten a little nudge from the jukebox, Gus recalled. And the woman entering the bar, Gwen Parker, who ran that store with the eclectic merchandise just a block up Seaview Avenue from Maeve's cookie shop... Last time Gwen had been inside the tavern, she and the actor had heard a song, too. Gus tried to recall what it was, but drew a blank. She did remember, though, that for the duration of a song, Gwen had ignored the guy she was with and stared at the movie guy. He'd stared at her, too.

Maybe the jukebox had nothing to do with it. He was mighty fine looking, even when he was unbarbered and unshaven. Any heterosexual woman would stare at him. Margie was certainly doing her share of staring right now.

All the staring in the world wouldn't help her. The movie guy smiled at Gwen's entrance and took a few steps toward her. They didn't hug in greeting, or shake hands, or touch in any way. Instead, they walked to one of the empty booths and sat facing each other. Gus was tempted to take their order herself, but she had tasks to attend to behind the bar. She signaled to one of the waitresses, who nodded, grabbed a refilled bowl of bar mix, and headed for their table.

Marge sighed, slid off her stool, and rummaged in her purse. She pulled out a quarter and grinned. "I guess I've got nothing to lose," she said.

"Except twenty-five cents." Gus waved in the direction of the jukebox. "Go ahead. Try your luck."

***

Dylan waited until the waitress had taken their order—a glass of chardonnay for Gwen, a Glenlivet neat for him—before he gave Gwen his full attention. Like him, she was damp from the rain, but she used a napkin to dry her face. She looked wary, her eyes not quite meeting his.

"How was your date?" he asked.

"Who said I had a date?" She carefully plucked several peanuts from the bowl of munchies on the table between them, tossed them into her mouth, chewed, swallowed.

"I assumed, since you weren't free for dinner." He scooped up a handful of pretzels, nuts, and cheese puffs from the bowl and thought about his uneaten dinner, back in his room at the Ocean Bluff Inn. "Are you free now? Where's Annie?"

"She's home with a babysitter." Gwen continued to watch him, her face giving nothing away.

"Well." His eyes remained on her as he nibbled the snacks in his hand. "I've bought a house."

"Here? In Brogan's Point?"

"A sprawling old Victorian in the northern end of town. I got word today that my bid was accepted. I've signed a contract. It's a beautiful house. It needs some updates, but it overlooks the ocean. It's got an incredible view."

Gwen shook her head. "I know you said you were thinking of doing this, but—it's so fast. You only just got here, and... Is this because of Annie?"

"I came to Brogan's Point because I needed a change. Running into you, and then learning about Annie—I had no idea. I didn't plan that. For all I knew, you could have moved away years ago." Her expression darkened slightly. He wasn't sure why. It wasn't as if they'd promised to stay in touch after that one night. "What happened six years ago—as far as I knew, that was nothing more than a happy memory. We both knew going in that it was a one-night thing. So no, I didn't follow up and find out if you were still living here six years later. That wasn't why I came."

Gwen remained silent as the waitress appeared with their drinks, and she shifted her attention to the pale liquid in her glass for a long moment. "It wasn't like me. That night, I mean. I never had a one-night stand before then. Or since."

"Because the one-night stand you had with me was so awful?"

Her eyes flashed with apology and—did he dare to hope?—amusement. "No. It was nice."

"It was awesome. On a ten point scale, it was a twenty."

She allowed herself a bashful smile. "Okay, it was *very* nice. But that's not who I am. I don't do things like that."

"You did things like that once."

"Because..." She lapsed into thought, sipping some wine. Dylan noticed that her fingernails were cut short and unpolished. As a single mother with a demanding career, he supposed she didn't have time for manicures. Once he was settled in Brogan's Point, he could make indulgences like manicures possible for her. He could take Annie for an afternoon or an evening so Gwen could spend time at a salon, without having to hire a sitter first.

"That night," she said, drawing his attention from her hands to her face, "I was just trying to forget a nasty break-up. I had wound up in Brogan's Point because that was where my college boyfriend found work. He was a math major, and he'd done student teaching as an undergrad. The high school here had lost a math teacher unexpectedly—some sort of family crisis, I don't remember. Anyway, they hired him, and while he taught, he studied for his master's degree at UMass Boston. Between his job and his schoolwork, he wasn't around much. I got a job at the Attic, and we found an apartment, and after a while, we started talking about marriage. But then..." She took another sip of wine. "He became involved with a classmate at UMass. When he finished his master's degree, he told me he was leaving me for her."

"He's nuts," Dylan said, partly because Gwen looked so vulnerable to him and partly because he believed it. As far as he could tell, Gwen was fantastic. How could anyone treat her like that?

"It was painful. I'd moved here for him and built my life around him, and suddenly he decided he didn't want to be with me anymore."

"What an asshole," Dylan said.

Another bashful smile flickered across her face. "Anyway, it was just a few weeks after he moved out that I met you. I was feeling like such a failure, like the kind of woman a guy would leave for someone else—and then you were so attentive, and you actually seemed to think I wasn't some pathetic reject—"

"Gwen. You are not a reject. And you're not pathetic." He reached across the table and gathered one of her hands in his. Her fingers were chilly. He hoped the warmth of his hand would spread to hers. "You were the coolest woman in the bar that night. You were gorgeous, and you had a dynamite smile, and you were friendly. You wanted to spend time with me. I thought I was the luckiest guy in the world."

"Equally lucky because I wasn't making any demands," she noted. "No strings. No ties. Just some fun sex. What guy can resist that?"

"I can." Her fingers did warm up. He felt them fluttering against his palm, and the sensation turned him on. "I do all the time. My manager is right—lots of women want to bang a movie star just for the hell of it. That kind of thing doesn't interest me."

"It interested you that night."

"You didn't want to bang a movie star. I wasn't a movie star then." He grinned. "I was a struggling actor working for union minimum on a no-budget flick. And you... You were earthy and funny and sexy. And you wanted me."

She lowered her eyes. "I did," she admitted.

"It was good," he reminded her.

She met his gaze. Along with bashfulness, he saw other wistfulness. Nostalgia. Yearning.

At least he hoped it was yearning. "We could have a night like that again."

"No, we couldn't." Her voice sounded a little rusty, the words not coming easily. "I'm a mother. I pay a babysitter by the hour to stay with my daughter. I don't get to go off to some man's bed for the night, just because I feel like it."

She felt like it. That was what Dylan came away with. "I can pay the babysitter."

"It's a school night."

"So you'll go home afterward. We'll just..." He gave her hand a little squeeze. "Relive some happy memories. I won't beg you to stay."

Her eyes flashed at those last words, and he felt something tug hard inside him, too. Why had he said that? He'd never begged a woman for anything, ever.

"It won't matter anyhow," she said, and he felt another tug. They were from the song, her words and his. The song about making love and then leaving. No strings.

He wanted to touch her cheek. But he didn't want her to leave. Not right now, anyway. Right now... He just wanted her.

And from the way she held his hand, the way she held his gaze, he knew she wanted him, too.

Chapter Fifteen

He told her he'd walked to the tavern; it was only a few short blocks from the Ocean Bluff Inn. So she drove them to the hotel in her car, through the misty drizzle.

She hoped her friend Monica wasn't behind the desk as they hurried up the porch steps and into the charming lobby, with its colonial furnishings and welcoming atmosphere. Monica's family owned the place, and Monica was working her way up, learning the business one job at a time. Fortunately, the night clerk behind the polished check-in desk was no one Gwen had ever seen before.

Dylan spirited her right past the desk to the broad, carpeted stairs and up to the second floor, then down the hall to a room at the end. It was smaller than she'd expected. Didn't movie stars stay in suites, with grand pianos and hot tubs big enough to contain an orgy?

This room was modest, with sturdy maple furniture and lacy drapes flanking the window. If there was a TV, it was hidden, probably behind the doors of the armoire across the room from the wide brass bed. An upholstered easy chair and ottoman occupied one corner, and a small writing table held an open laptop and a folder of papers. Atop a wheeled cart sat a plate covered with a silver lid and a glass of ice water—the remnants of a room service meal, Gwen guessed. She glimpsed a pair of flip-flops just beyond the threshold separating the bedroom from the bathroom, and a flannel shirt was draped over the knob of the closet door, but otherwise, the room was reasonably tidy.

Dylan closed the door, then placed his hands on her shoulders and eased her around to face him. "You okay with this?" he asked.

Funny, she didn't recall him asking her that the last time she'd accompanied him to his room. That had been a cheap motel, not a pretty ocean-front inn overflowing with ambiance. And he hadn't had to ask that time. They'd been all over each other.

She wanted to be all over him now. He stood before her, tall and lean, his eyes smoky with desire. His lips curved in a question. His hands remained on her shoulders, light but warm, holding but not clinging.

"Yes," she murmured. "I'm okay."

He bowed and touched his mouth to hers, a gentle brush, asking in its own way whether she was okay. She answered by circling her arms around him, flattening her hands against his broad, strong back, and opening her mouth to him.

Clearly, that was the answer he'd been waiting for. He hauled her close, the fingers of one hand digging into her hair while his other hand moved down her spine to her waist. His tongue slid deep, taking possession of her mouth, claiming it. She felt just as crazed as she had that night so many years ago, just as hungry for him, just as delirious with arousal. She'd been with two men in her life whom she'd considered marrying, and neither of them had ever made her feel what Dylan made her feel: sheer, unadulterated lust.

He pulled at her sweater. She tugged at his shirt. He kicked off one shoe, then slid his hands to her bottom and lifted her off her feet. She wrapped her legs around his waist and he carried her to the bed, never once breaking the kiss.

They tumbled together onto the fluffy down comforter, yanking at each other's clothing and their own. Gwen wriggled out of her sweater, and Dylan unfastened her bra and tossed it over the side of the bed. She unbuttoned his shirt, and he shrugged out of it and hurled it across the room. He worked open the zipper of her slacks and slid the garment down her legs, dragging her panties along. Thank goodness they were too busy kissing for him to pay any attention to her underwear, which was strictly practical and pathetically unsexy. As a single mother, Gwen had no time—and no budget—for elegant lingerie.

Not that Dylan noticed, or cared. Once he'd disposed of her slacks, he writhed out of his jeans. Then he slowed, pausing in his kisses to lean back on his haunches and gaze at her naked body. It wasn't the same body he'd seen so long ago. It was six years older, and it had endured a pregnancy. Her breasts had nourished her baby. Her skin had been stretched, her hips stressed. She never wasted time obsessing about the changes Annie had wrought, because Annie was so worth it. Gwen would have willingly sacrificed a leg in exchange for the blessing of having Annie in her life. A few stretch marks and a bit of saggy, baggy flesh didn't matter.

Apparently, they didn't matter to Dylan, either. He bowed to kiss one breast and then the other, then cupped his hands around them and squeezed gently. "You are so beautiful," he murmured.

She recalled the line about beauty being in the eyes of the beholder—and her beholder's eyes were beautiful. All of Dylan was truly beautiful. The shadow of his beard made his chin look sharper, his cheekbones more chiseled. His mouth was determined. His hair was wild with waves. She tangled her fingers through the locks, turned on by their silky texture.

But then, everything about Dylan turned her on—his hair, his dark, intense gaze, his broad shoulders and slender hips and long legs. His muscles had more definition than she remembered. He wasn't bulky, but he was definitely buff. He'd probably had to undergo extensive fitness training for his cinematic stints as Captain Steele.

She slid her hands from his hair down his back, his skin warm and sleek beneath her palms. He let her touch him as he touched her, grazing her throat, sweeping his tongue down the hollow between her breasts, caressing her thighs and stroking the damp heat between them. When she moaned, he stopped and pushed away. "I've got condoms," he said. "Unless you want to make another baby."

Her first thought was *yes!* But then she realized that *yes* only meant yes, she wanted him. She wanted him inside her. She wanted him to rock and roll her, to do sinful things to her, to deliver her to ecstasy and then join her there. But no, she didn't want another child. Not now, not with him. This was about one night, like the last time. This was letting go, drowning in sensation. It wasn't about creating a family and signing on for twenty years of responsibility.

She couldn't get pregnant, anyway; she had an IUD. But he was a Hollywood celebrity with a no doubt active sex life. "Go get your condoms," she said, her voice so thick with yearning she almost didn't recognize it.

He sprang off the bed, sprinted into the bathroom, and returned with a box, which he tore open en route. And then he was back in her arms, sprawled on top of her, kissing her, pressing into her. Finally, *finally* filling her.

They peaked too quickly, but it didn't matter. Her orgasm was so sharp it almost hurt, but that didn't matter, either. She closed her eyes and rode it out, accepting it for what it was. One time. One encounter with this amazing man.

She had to go home. It was a school night; she needed to send Hayley back to her own house at a reasonable time, or Hayley's mother would stop letting her babysit for Gwen.

But she didn't want to leave just yet. Her head was nestled deep into the soft down pillows, but she was able to turn it enough to glimpse her watch. Eight-forty. She could stay with Dylan a little longer. Lying in the warmth of his embrace, his body aggressive and protective at the same time, felt too good.

He eased off her, settling his head next to hers on the pillow and drawing her against him. "What is it with us?" he asked. "Chemistry or something?"

"Maybe." She smiled and the motion caused her mouth to brush against the heated skin beneath his collarbone. That Dylan found their lovemaking as spectacular as she did reassured her, even if she was mystified by it. She was no great lover. She hadn't had a lot of practice with a lot of men. Yet with him...

Chemistry. Or something.

"It was phenomenal last time, too," he said, stroking his fingers lazily through her hair. "We shouldn't wait six years to do it again."

If he moved to Brogan's Point, they wouldn't have to wait six years. He'd be a short drive away. They could see each other whenever they wanted. They could *date*. God, that sounded so juvenile, especially after they'd set the world on fire with sex.

Did movie stars even date? Did they call women up and ask them to...what? Go to the movies? That seemed too self-referential.

In any case, why would Dylan want to date her? He was famous. He could have any woman he wanted. She owned a little shop in a little town. She liked her quiet life—and in fact, many days, when Annie was a handful and the store was plagued by hassles and snafus, she wished her life was even quieter. Her idea of success was a day with good sales and some time spent cuddling with her daughter while they read a bedtime story. Her idea of glamor was dangly earrings and a slick of lipstick. Her idea of fame was winning the Good Citizen award from the Brogan's Point Business Council because of her efforts to get recycle bins placed next to the trash cans on Seaview and Atlantic Avenues.

The first time Dylan had made love to her, he hadn't been successful or glamorous or famous, at least not the way he was now. Perhaps this time was about nostalgia, or about the discovery that, thanks to Annie, he was inextricably linked to Gwen. But really, this wasn't a *relationship*. It couldn't be.

"I should go," she said.

She felt his arms relent. He eased away from her, pushed himself to sit, and gazed down at her. "I want you to see the house," he said. "I want you to tell me if you think Annie will like it."

She sighed, fighting off a sudden pang of grief. If Dylan lived in Brogan's Point, she would lose Annie. Not fully, not the way she would if Dylan put his money and power behind a full-fledged custody battle. She doubted he wanted custody. That possibility didn't concern her.

But if he settled into a house nearby and encouraged Annie to visit him whenever she wanted, they would develop a bond, one that eroded Gwen's own exclusive bond with her daughter.

It would be good for Annie. But not necessarily for Gwen.

"I'd drive you home, but you've got your car here."

"It's not a problem." If this were a date, of course, he'd expect to see her back to her house. But it wasn't a date. It was...a flash of fireworks on a dismal, drizzly evening.

She forced herself off the bed. The room wasn't cold, but the more distance she put between herself and Dylan, the chillier she felt.

She wasn't a swoony romantic. She knew this interlude hadn't been about true love. She'd stopped believing in true love the day Adam told her he'd fallen for someone else and was leaving her.

But she *wanted* to believe. She *wanted* to think that what she'd just experienced with Dylan meant something.

While she got dressed, he pulled on his boxer briefs. Too much of him remained visible—the supple contours of his chest, the narrow punctuation of his navel, the sinewy muscles in his arms and legs. His face. His eyes, still dark with hunger as he watched her put on her bra, her pants, her sweater.

When she was dressed, he crossed to her, gave her a gentle hug, and kissed her brow. "I'll call you," he said.

She nodded, fighting off ridiculous waves of sorrow. *This doesn't mean anything,* she reminded herself as she touched her lips to his cheek. But she was afraid to say anything, afraid that instead of words, she'd release a sob. So she only turned and walked away.

Chapter Sixteen

The inspection went well. The roof had at least another ten years of life in it, there was no dry rot or insect damage, the appliances were all functioning and the septic system was up to code. Since Dylan didn't need a mortgage to finance the house's purchase, he saw no reason to delay the deal.

His agent did. "Are you sure you want to do this?" Brian asked when Dylan phoned him later after the inspector had left. "You want to spend a winter in New England?"

"I grew up in Nebraska," Dylan reminded him. "I know how to drive in the snow."

"It all just seems a little drastic," Brian argued. "Your work is here in L.A. Your life is here."

No, Dylan thought. *My life is in Brogan's Point.* His daughter was there. His daughter's mother was there. "It's not like I'm on another planet," Dylan said. "We can still talk."

"Only because I'm willing to wake up at the crack of dawn. Time zones, Dylan. Three damned hours difference."

It was eleven a.m. in Massachusetts, eight a.m. in California. Not exactly the crack of dawn.

"You left in a huff. You were pissed about *The Angel.* But you know the nature of the business. You're a big success. You've got this city falling at your feet. You don't need to live three thousand miles away."

"I don't need to live there, either." And somehow, Dylan felt, he *did* need to live in Brogan's Point—where he had a daughter. And that daughter's mother.

He'd wanted to contact Gwen when the inspection was done, to let her know it had gone well. But he'd called Brian instead, because Gwen, unlike Los Angeles, wasn't falling at his feet. Last night had been incredible—and afterward, she'd just walked away.

Sure, it was a school night, and the baby sitter had to be dealt with. He'd dated a mother once before, a stunning actress who had a toddler. She'd also had a full-time nanny, a sixty-year-old Ecuadorian immigrant named Consuela, so staying out late on a school night, or spending the night in Dylan's bed, had never been an issue.

The truth was, he had no idea what dealing with baby sitters entailed. Being a parent meant a lot more than playing with Legos and sitting through a kiddie flick. Hell, he didn't even know how to talk to a five-year-old girl after the movie was over.

He could learn, though. He could learn, if Gwen would let him. If she didn't erect a barrier between him and Annie the way she'd seemingly erected one between him and herself last night.

He thought about phoning her, but he didn't want to interrupt her at work. He thought about texting her, but she might not check her messages for hours. He decided to visit her store, with a stop at that cookie bakery on the way.

He arrived at the Attic bearing a box filled with an assortment of cookies for her and her staff. She wasn't at the cash register when he entered, but he did spot an end-cap display of ketchup and mustard bottles with the goofy "Squeeze Pleeze" slogan scrawled across their curving red and yellow surfaces. He lifted a cellophane-wrapped package containing the bottle set. They would go well with the old-but-functioning appliances in his kitchen.

The young woman who rang up his purchase looked familiar. He must have met her on his last visit to Gwen's store. Her smile as she waited for his credit card to process implied that she recognized him, too. But then, she might recognize him from the Galaxy Force movies and not from a previous encounter.

He accepted the bag with his squeeze bottles and set the box of cookies on the counter. "Is Gwen in?" he asked. "These cookies are for her and the whole staff here."

"Gwen is into healthy food," the woman said with a rueful smile. "But *I* love cookies. Especially Maeve Nolan's cookies."

"They're pretty special," he agreed. "So...is Gwen around?"

"She's in her office. Let me see if she's available." She lifted a phone, tapped a few buttons, and held it to her ear. "Hey, Gwen? That actor is here and he wants to see you. He brought cookies." She listened for a moment, laughed, and set down the phone. "She'll be out in a minute."

"What did she say that was so funny?" he asked.

The woman shrugged. "She said, 'Thank god he didn't bring flowers.' I guess that's not so funny." She laughed again.

Dylan wasn't sure if it was funny, either. He stepped away from the counter and closed his eyes. As an actor, he was adept at imagining himself in other settings, other scenes, and he had no trouble imagining himself in bed with Gwen, the way they were last night. He imagined her silky skin against his fingertips, her breasts against his lips, her body tight and pulsing around him.

Why had she bolted? What was she afraid of?

An elderly couple entered the store, hand in hand, the woman expounding on the adorable sunhat she'd bought at the Attic last summer, the man muttering that no one needed a sunhat at this time of year. They bickered affectionately, the way people who'd been married forever did. Dylan's parents were like that. They could spar for an hour over which one of them had suggested that they plant azaleas beside the front porch. Those silly spats were a kind of lovemaking.

Would he ever be with one woman long enough to reach that comfort level? Would he ever be an old married man holding hands with a gray-haired woman and arguing about sunhats?

Would that woman be a fellow actor, someone elegant and glamorous, as rich and successful as he was? Or would she be a modest store owner in a seaside New England town?

Gwen's appearance didn't answer that question. With her hair pulled into a pony-tail and her face devoid of make-up, she sure didn't look elegant or glamorous. Her eyes were wary as her gaze met his, and they were underlined with shadow. Had she had trouble sleeping last night?

He grinned at her, and she responded with a tenuous smile. "Hey," he said.

"You brought cookies?"

He gestured toward the box on the counter. "That cookie store down the street? The baker is worse than a crack dealer."

"Her cookies are good," Gwen agreed.

"Are you free for dinner tonight?"

She shifted her gaze from his face to the bag in his hand, to the shelf of wooden puzzles beside her, to the end-cap with the squeeze bottles, then back to him. "I'm spending this evening with Annie."

"Can we all have dinner together?" If he was going to learn how to be a father to the little girl, he could start by spending the evening with her, too.

"Dylan." Gwen took a step closer to him and lowered her voice. "I don't know... Last night—"

"—was last night," he cut her off. He didn't want to give her a chance to say no. "Today is today. I'm here. We need to make this work."

She pressed her lips together, clearly not pleased. "*This?*" Her voice remained hushed and taut. "There is no *this*."

"There's Annie."

"She's not a *this*."

"She's my daughter," he said. He kept his voice as muted as hers, but he glanced toward the counter just to make sure the clerk there couldn't hear their conversation. He'd be happy to run up a flag on the town green proclaiming that he was Annie's father, but Gwen obviously wasn't ready to go public with the relationship. And with him, a flag would only be the start of it. The tabloids would go nuts with the news. Some photographer would snap a hideous picture of him holding

Annie, and it would appear in all the supermarket rags with the headline, "Captain Steele's Love Child." There would be an inset photo of Gwen, looking grim and drab, pony-tail and no make-up.

He was used to that crap. When he'd chosen a high-profile film career, he'd known an unwelcome publicity might be part of it. Gwen hadn't asked for that, though. She deserved her privacy.

As resentful as she looked right now, she also looked vulnerable. He wanted to gather her into his arms and reassure her. He wanted to promise her that he'd protect her and Annie from the paparazzi and every other threat to their wellbeing, that he'd be a positive addition to their lives. He was a decent guy. He'd do the best he could.

He wanted to take her in his arms—but he wanted more than just to reassure her. Yes, he was a decent guy—but he wanted to press her to himself, to nuzzle the sexy hollow of her throat, nibble the skin beneath her ear, fill his hands with her lush, round breasts.

He wanted so much. No wonder she looked apprehensive.

After a long, tense minute, she sighed. "You can stop by after dinner," she said. "I need some time alone with my daughter this evening."

"I'll come at seven," he said. He wanted to get to Gwen's house while Annie was still awake. Bonding with Annie was more important than bonding with Gwen, he acknowledged. Last night notwithstanding, Gwen had a guy in her life. Maybe she loved the guy; maybe that was why she was behaving so skittish now. She might be riven with guilt for having cheated on her boyfriend.

But whether or not Gwen was involved with someone else, Annie was still Dylan's daughter. No boyfriend could change that.

Besides, if Dylan showed up at Gwen's house after Annie was asleep, he'd be tempted to do something that would make Gwen feel even guiltier. Alone with her, Dylan would want to make love again. Slowly. Softly, so they wouldn't wake Annie up. They'd have to stifle their groans, suppress their cries. That would make the whole thing even more intense.

Just thinking about it made him hot.

Definitely, he'd go when Annie was still awake, and hope a five-year-old chaperone would be able to put a lid on his lust.

***

Annie was bubbling like a pot of boiling water when Gwen picked her up from her after-school program. "We had this art teacher come today," she reported once they were in the car, heading home. "She teaches art at the community center where I swim. She had us make...I'm trying to remember what it's called. We glued cotton balls and ribbons and yarn on pieces of cardboard. And other stuff, too. Popsicle sticks. And this stuff that felt like leather but she said it wasn't."

"That's called a collage," Gwen told her, eyeing her daughter in the rear-view mirror as she drove.

Annie nodded enthusiastically. "That's it! Collages. We made collages. Can I take her class at the community center? I love art. I want to be an artist when I grow up."

"I thought you wanted to be a dentist," Gwen reminded her. That was what Annie had said after her last dental check-up, when the technician had cleaned her teeth with bubble-gum flavored polish and presented her with a toothbrush that had a sparkly handle.

"I can be both," Annie declared. "A dentist and an artist. And I'll have a dog, too."

Her future sounded busy.

Once home, they set to work in the kitchen. Annie, in her Winnie-the-Pooh apron, tore romaine lettuce into a salad bowl while Gwen seasoned a chicken breast and slid it into the oven to broil. She felt safe in her own home, away from Mike, away from Dylan.

Coming clean to Mike hadn't been a mistake; that had been the right thing to do, even though the truth had irreparably damaged their relationship. Making love with Dylan, though—that had been a huge mistake. She wasn't young and carefree anymore. She couldn't afford to behave so recklessly. She had responsibilities now.

More than behaving recklessly, she couldn't afford to be so distracted, the way she'd been today. All day long, her thoughts had been invaded by erotic memories, flashes of arousal triggered unexpectedly. Sorting through invoices in her office, she'd suddenly remembered the way Dylan's tongue had felt flicking against her skin, and her thigh muscles had clenched painfully. Hanging a few mobiles above the counter, where they'd be sure to capture the attention of shoppers, she'd recalled the sensation of floating and drifting after she'd come. She'd remembered how hard Dylan had been, how strong, how deliciously heavy he'd felt on top of her, inside her.

She couldn't have those thoughts. They undermined her concentration. They shattered her equilibrium.

As she cut broccoli into a bowl of water to be microwaved, she glanced over at her daughter. Annie was so innocent. Gwen swore to herself that she was entitled to her own adult pleasures, but in the presence of her spunky, beguiling daughter, she felt unworthy and sordid.

She filled a glass with water for herself, and Annie's favorite sippy cup with milk, and they settled at the table to eat. Annie rattled on for a while about her school day. The teacher had read a story about farms, and then they learned how to sound out some relevant words: barn, cow, pig, corn. These were easy words, Annie said. Gwen noted that the farm didn't grow any multisyllabic crops—sorghum or alfalfa or pomegranates.

"Annie," she said once the little girl had wound down. "There's something we need to talk about."

Annie gave her a wide-eyed look.

"You know that man, Dylan Scott, who we went to the movie with?"

"And we had pizza with him," Annie reminded her. "And I played Legos with him. And he gave me a book."

"Right."

"He's fun," Annie said. "Can we see him again?"

"He'll be coming over in a little while," Gwen told her.

"Can we play Legos again?"

"If it isn't too late. Here's what we need to talk about, though." Gwen wished her water was a glass of wine, but she needed her wits about her to get through this conversation. "He's your daddy."

Annie's eyes grew wider. Gwen gazed at her wild mop of hair, as dark and wavy as her father's. Her eyes were Dylan's, too. Gwen could lay claim to Annie's mouth and chin. Her nose was still a cute little button, resembling neither Gwen's nor Dylan's.

"How come?" Annie finally asked.

"How come what?"

"How come he's my daddy? He doesn't even live here."

"He was here before you were born. He and I were friends. But he left before I even knew I was pregnant with you, and I couldn't reach him. So he didn't know about you until he came back."

"He should have come back sooner," Annie said reasonably.

"Well, he couldn't. He was busy working."

"You work, and you're here."

"Yes, but that's because I'm your mommy. I'll always be here for you."

Annie poked at her broccoli with her fork as she mulled over Gwen's promise. "My daddy won't always be here for me," she concluded.

Her words pierced Gwen's heart, not just because they expressed a rock-solid truth as Annie understood it, but because they expressed Gwen's greatest fear. Dylan was here now, but he could leave at any moment. He was buying a house in Brogan's Point, but he could afford to buy houses all over the world, and live wherever he wanted. He could make love with Gwen one night and leave the next day. He didn't make promises. And even if he did, Gwen had no reason to believe him.

The doorbell rang. Gwen checked her watch: seven o'clock. At least he could be relied on to show up on time.

Annie bolted from her chair. "That's him!" she shouted. "That's my daddy! Can we play Legos?"

Gwen raced after her daughter, who reached the front door and hovered impatiently, her hand on the doorknob. Gwen peeked through the window in the door and nodded her permission. Annie swung the door open.

Dylan stood on the porch, looking ridiculously sexy in his worn jeans and his leather jacket. He held a small bag with the Cookie's logo on it. "You already brought me cookies today," she said disapprovingly.

"That was for your staff. These are for Annie," he said, handing the bag to the child. "I'm getting addicted to the cookies from that store."

Annie's face radiated joy. "Can I have them, Mommy?"

"You can have one," Gwen said, not exactly thrilled. She didn't want Dylan bearing gifts every time he saw Annie, as if he was trying to buy her affection.

"You're my daddy," Annie informed him as she unrolled the top of the bag and peered inside. She pulled out a cookie and obediently handed the bag to Gwen, who rolled the top back up, her way of signaling that Annie wouldn't get any more cookies tonight.

The little girl scampered back to the kitchen, clutching her precious cookie. She knew she'd have to finish her broccoli before she'd be allowed to devour the treat. Gwen watched her go, then turned to Dylan. He stepped inside, gaping at her, his expression troubled. "You told her?"

"Yes."

"I thought... I don't know, I thought we'd tell her together."

Gwen shook her head. If they'd presented this news to Annie as a team, she would perceive them as just that: a team. A twosome. United.

Gwen had feared, when Dylan first showed up in town, that he might try to steal Annie from her if he knew she was his daughter. She still harbored those misgivings. She was determined to maintain her position as the primary parent, the one who told her daughter all the important things. She and Dylan were *not* a team.

"What did she think?" he asked.

She thinks you're going to leave. "She's processing it," Gwen told him. "She wants you to play Legos with her."

He looked relieved. But rather than chase after his daughter, he cupped his hand around her cheek. "We can do this," he said, sounding so sure of himself, she was tempted to believe him. "Last night meant something. Annie means everything. We can make this work. Okay?"

He was a good actor. So persuasive, so convincing. And really, she had no reason *not* to believe him, other than the fact that he was rich and famous and mind-bogglingly successful, charismatic and unreasonably handsome, and she was a single mother who worked her tail off to make a modest life for her daughter and herself. And the fact that, despite last night, and despite that night six years ago, she and Dylan hardly knew each other.

And the fact that she could fall in love with him—which could be the worst mistake she'd ever made.

Chapter Seventeen

Saturday afternoon, he took Gwen and Annie to see the house.

It wasn't his yet. Even without the delay of applying for a mortgage, the process of transferring ownership of the property took time. The deed had to be authenticated. A lawyer had to ascertain that there were no liens on the property. T's had to be crossed, i's dotted.

But Dylan was already thinking about it as *his* house. Sometimes, he even thought about it as *their* house—his and Annie's and Gwen's.

He'd had to wait until Saturday afternoon to show it to them. Gwen worked weekdays and Saturday mornings. Dylan kept himself busy during the days, conferring with Brian on licensing deals, reviewing promotional schedules for the upcoming Galaxy Force film, which was scheduled for release on Memorial Day weekend, and haggling with the screenwriters over issues he had on the next Galaxy Force film, which was slated to start filming early in the new year. He had to admit that Brian had a point: dealing long-distance with these things and accommodating the three-hour time difference made his job harder than it would have been if he were living in California. But he'd sworn to Gwen that they could make this work, and he was determined.

He'd spent every evening with Gwen and Annie, at least. He wasn't used to cooking, but he'd asked Gwen for a shopping list and driven to a supermarket on Route One, sparing her a chore and contributing to her pantry. If she was going to include him in her dinners, the least he could do was help pay for them.

Of course, he'd have preferred to do much more. If she'd let him, he would have hired a cook for her, someone who could do all the shopping and food preparation so she wouldn't have to do that herself. But he didn't dare to suggest it. Gwen was a proud woman. She would have taken such a gesture as presumptuous, the actions of an arrogant rich guy throwing his money around.

So instead, he'd bought potatoes and fresh tuna steaks—an indulgence she could rarely afford, she'd admitted to him—and a basket of locally grown apples. He'd peeled and cored the apples while she and Annie had prepared a pie crust. Annie had wielded the rolling pin like a pro. "I want to be a chef when I grow up," she'd announced, and when Gwen had reminded her that she also wanted to be a dentist and an artist, she'd insisted that she could be all three.

He and Gwen didn't have sex again. Every evening, he would play with Annie or read to her or watch a video with her, and then Gwen would take over, giving Annie her bath and tucking her into bed while Dylan tidied up the kitchen or caught up on emails or otherwise sat around idly. He was willing to help out with Annie's bedtime—not the bath, of course, but the tucking in, the bedtime story, the quiet, intimate moments when a parent might plant a dream seed or two. But he respected Gwen's desire to have that time alone with her daughter. He knew he was an imposition on them. He didn't want to encroach even more.

So he'd wait until Gwen descended the stairs alone, having launched her daughter into slumber-land. He'd give Gwen a hug, a kiss or two—and he'd sense her withdrawal. He'd see desire in her eyes but feel fear in her body.

"I won't hurt you," he vowed on Friday night. He'd kissed her, and she'd returned his kiss for a luscious moment before pulling back and stepping away from him.

"You don't know what you'll do," she responded.

"Can you trust me?"

"Can you give me some time?"

He understood. He had to earn her trust. Patience wasn't his long suit, but for her—and for Annie—he'd be patient.

He was glad she's agreed to visit his house with Annie on Saturday afternoon. He'd arranged with Andrea to meet them at the house with the key, and the four of them entered the house together. Both Gwen and Annie appeared awed by the size of the entry foyer. The great room beyond impressed them even more. "Look, Mommy!" Annie had crowed. "This is so big! I can run around here." She extended her arms as if they were wings, and sprinted in loopy circles around the empty room.

"She runs around in our house, too," Gwen muttered. But Dylan knew Annie couldn't run so swiftly or so freely in their cozy little house, not without crashing into the walls.

"Look at this," Annie continued, racing to the fieldstone fireplace. "It's bigger than me! You could build a fire and roast marshmallows. My friend Lucy has a fireplace," she added for Dylan's benefit. "Her mommy doesn't let us roast marshmallows in it, though. She says they'll drip on the floor and make mess."

"She's also afraid you'll get hurt," Gwen reminded Annie. "You have to stay behind the screen, or you can get burned."

"I'm careful. I love roasted marshmallows." Annie did another arm-flapping turn around the living room, her sneakers squeaking against the polished wood floor.

"Want to see the kitchen?" Dylan asked Gwen.

Andrea had been quietly observing Dylan, Gwen, and Annie, her expression a mix of bemusement and calculation. No doubt she was trying to figure out what Dylan had to do with the owner of the Attic and her rambunctious daughter. But she apparently felt the kitchen was a subject for women, and she spoke up. "It's a bit outdated, but I think you'll see it has enormous potential."

Gwen arched an eyebrow and followed Andrea past the formal dining room to the spacious kitchen.

Dylan understood that arched eyebrow and the sentiment behind it. Andrea seemed to think Gwen would be in charge of the kitchen. She'd reached the assumption that this house would signify something to Gwen, that Gwen would have some say in enabling the kitchen to reach its potential.

Dylan would like nothing more than for Gwen to design the kitchen to meet her needs and wants. He'd happily hand her a blank check and tell her to go crazy. Six-burner professional gas stove. Sub-zero refrigerator. Temperature-controlled wine rack. Two sinks, one against the wall and one in the center island. Counters of granite, engineered stone, marble, whatever she wanted.

But he couldn't even get her to sleep with him. Allowing him to coronate her queen of the kitchen implied much more of a commitment than simply having sex with him.

Gwen wandered around the kitchen, angling her head to scrutinize the sink, craning her neck to inspect the vent above the stove. "This is the biggest kitchen in the world," Annie announced as she pranced through the doorway. "It's bigger than the kitchen in a castle. It's *giant*."

"I don't think it's the biggest kitchen in the world," Gwen told her.

"It's bigger than our kitchen."

"By a bit," Gwen agreed.

"By a lot. It's so big, you could have a party here. The biggest party in the world."

Dylan appreciated her enthusiasm. "Come on, Annie—I'll show you upstairs." He took Annie's hand and ushered her past the pantry to the back stairs. Behind him, he heard Andrea say, "Dylan has discussed some of his ideas for renovating this kitchen, but I'm sure you'll want some input, too."

"No, that's all right," Gwen responded. "It's his kitchen." He imagined that must have bemused Andrea even more.

He should have U-turned, stomped back down to the kitchen and told Gwen this kitchen could be hers if she wanted it. The whole house could be hers. She could made the decorating decisions. She could choose the furniture, the fixtures. She could dress up the place with objects from her store. A framed mirror in the foyer. A pewter vase on the dining room table. A captain's clock on the fireplace mantel. A colorful silk scarf looped over a door knob. "Squeeze Pleeze" bottles on the kitchen counter. He still had the set he'd bought in his room at the Ocean Bluff Inn, but he would display them prominently on the kitchen counter.

Whatever Gwen wanted. Blank check, carte blanche. His only goal was for her to feel comfortable about this house. And about him.

But Annie had already raced to the top of the stairs and swept into one of the bedrooms. "This is the biggest bedroom!" she shouted. "I can see the ocean!"

That can be your bedroom, Annie, he thought as he chased after her.

*

What struck Gwen most forcefully about the house was not its size or its location but the fact that Dylan was sharing it with her.

She had tried all week to maintain a dignified distance from him—and she thought she'd been reasonably successful. He'd been doing everything right: playing with Annie, talking with her, forging a relationship with her, and all the while respecting the boundaries Gwen had established. He didn't try to spoil Annie, or to undermine Gwen's discipline. He questioned Annie about school and looked as if he actually cared about her answers. Gwen still couldn't quite believe he wanted to settle in this quaint New England town and be a quaint New England dad, attending soccer games and volunteering for carpools, debating lawn care products with the neighbors and sitting through town meeting every spring.

She sensed that sharing his house with her was his way of convincing her that, yes, he was ready to be a typical suburban father. Not that there was anything typical about Dylan... But it was clear that Gwen's opinion of the house mattered to him.

The real estate agent's chatter implied that she saw things that way. "I know of some terrific contractors who could redo the cabinets here," she said, gesturing around the kitchen. "New countertops, new appliances—this could be a true chef's kitchen."

"I wonder if Dylan could be a true chef," Gwen said, not adding that Annie was the Parker female aiming toward true chef-dom, along with all her other career aspirations.

The agent faltered for a moment. "Well, I suppose men enjoy cooking as much as women do," she said, a feeble nod toward sexual equality. "Would you like to see the master bedroom?"

Gwen would like to see the bedroom Annie was screeching about, a bedroom apparently large enough to hold Red Sox games inside. But unfortunately, she also wanted to see the master bedroom. She wanted to see the room where Dylan would sleep at night. The room where his long, strong body would sprawl across a big, comfortable bed. A room where a woman could find herself sprawled out beside him, his arms wrapped possessively around her.

Much as she'd hoped to resist him, Gwen was falling hard for Dylan. He was everything he was supposed to be, everything she could ask for. A father for Annie. A partner for her. Quiet and low-key, yet endowed with a firm will and a determination to get what he was after, to accomplish his goals. To win.

He was smart. He was successful. He was gorgeous.

He wanted her. He probably knew she wanted him, too, but he didn't push or pressure her—which only made her want him more.

A week wasn't long enough for her to know what to do about him. It wasn't long enough to know what she felt about him. But her feelings didn't wear a watch. They were divorced from time. And they told her that having Dylan in her life—and Annie's—would be a lot nicer than shutting him out.

The master bedroom was lovely, just as Gwen had expected it would be. It had broad windows along one wall that offered a glorious view of the grassy slope that descended from the house's patio to a stretch of sand and the ocean beyond. She imagined waking up early and pulling back the curtains to watch the sun rise out of the sea.

She imagined waking up early and finding Dylan beside her.

Dylan was certain he and she could make this thing work. Bit by bit, his certainty was rubbing off on her.

Chapter Eighteen

That evening, Gwen suggested that they spend a quiet night at her house. Over a dinner of take-out Chinese, they discussed Dylan's house. Not surprisingly, Annie was full of suggestions. She believed the back yard needed a swing set, and the den should have lots of built-in book cases and also an easel so she could paint there. When Gwen proposed that the finished rec room in the basement might be a better place for her to do her painting, Annie argued that once Dylan installed a pool table, a Ping-Pong table, and an electric train set in the rec room, there would be no space for an easel.

After dinner, Dylan sat at the kitchen table with Annie, teaching her the finer points of gin rummy while Gwen packed up the leftovers and wedged them into the refrigerator. Then she joined the game, everyone playing with their cards spread face-up so Dylan could give Annie guidance. "You don't want to discard your five of hearts," he explained. "You've got the six of hearts. You might draw the four or the seven and have a meld. Which card do you think you should get rid of?"

"The queen?"

"Right. She's no use to you."

"But she's a queen!"

"So's your mother. You've already got a queen," Dylan said, shooting Gwen an adorable smile.

"That means I'm a princess," Annie said, plucking the queen from her arrayed cards and putting it on the discard pile. "When I grow up, I want to be a queen. And a dentist," she added, nodding to Gwen.

"And an artist and a chef?" Gwen asked.

"Not a chef. I decided. Queens don't cook. They have people cook for them."

"You got that right," Dylan said, as Gwen simultaneously groaned, "Uh-oh."

They played cards until it was time for Annie's bath. As Gwen shuttled in and out of the bathroom, checking on Annie as the little girl sailed an armada of toys through the bath water, she felt a shimmering sense of wellbeing settle over her. She'd been resisting Dylan because she'd doubted his commitment to creating a family with her and Annie, but her doubt was gradually being washed away like beach sand carried off by the tides. Any man gentle enough to teach a five-year-old the finer points of gin rummy deserved to be a part of that five-year-old's life.

Why resist? Everything would be so much better if she let Dylan be a real father to Annie.

Once bath time had ended and Annie had donned her nightgown and brushed her teeth, Gwen tucked her into bed. She read a Curious George book, then kissed her daughter's forehead, turned out the light, and closed the door.

Dylan was seated in the living room, reading something on his cell phone. He glanced up when Gwen entered the room. "Anything important?" she asked with a nod toward the phone.

"Nah. Just Brian, asking on the status of the house."

"What did you tell him?"

"I told him you liked it," Dylan said, measuring Gwen's reaction with his gaze. "I hope you don't make a liar out of me."

"I liked it," she assured him with a smile. "It's very big."

"Big enough for three."

"Big enough for a visiting army," she joked, crossing to the credenza and opening a cabinet. He hadn't come right out and said he wanted her and Annie living in the house with him, and she wouldn't make that assumption. She would wait until he asked. "Would you like to watch a movie?"

"Sure." He tossed his phone onto the end table and settled back on the sofa cushions.

She pulled her DVD of *Sea Glass* from the rack and inserted it into the DVD player. Then she joined him on the sofa, dimming the lamp to make the screen images clearer.

As soon as Dylan recognized the movie, he swore. She hit pause and looked at him. "Do you not want to watch this?"

"No, I do. It's been a while since I've seen it." He considered, then corrected himself. "More than a while."

"Then why did you curse?"

"I love this movie." He sighed and stared at Gwen. "I loved the script. I loved making it. Obviously, I loved filming here in Brogan's Point. I loved everything about it." He took her hand. "I loved that night we spent together."

"And viewing the movie makes you want to curse?"

He laughed and shook his head. "Seeing the movie reminds me of how much I want to be making movies like that. Not Galaxy Force movies. I want to make quiet movies, movies with realistic characters and human stories. And I can't do that anymore."

"Of course you can."

"No. I can't." He dropped his gaze to their hands and traced his thumb back and forth over her palm as he spoke. "I wanted to be in an artistic, small-scale movie named *The Angel* that's in pre-production now. I read the script and loved it. I loved the main character in it. He's a guy who was always perfectly well-behaved in life, practically a saint. And he dies, and he becomes an angel, and God says, 'Now that you're an angel, what is your wish?' And his wish is to be bad. He just wants to cut loose a little. So he gets the chance to go back to earth and be a son of a bitch for a little while."

"It sounds kind of funny," Gwen said.

"It is. It's a comedy, but poignant. No slapstick. No big visual gags. It's a thought-provoking story about whether we get more satisfaction by being good than by being bad. But it's got some laughs in it, too."

He sandwiched her hand between both of his. The warmth of his touch spread through her, soothing and arousing her at the same time. She treasured not just their physical nearness but his words, his voice, the information he was imparting to her.

"Anyway, I told Brian I wanted the part. He talked to the producers. They said, 'What are you, crazy? He's Captain Steele.'"

"You should have fought for the part."

"Oh, I did. I fought. Brian fought. I practically memorized the script, and Brian got me an audition. And I blew them away."

Gwen smiled, then let her smile wane when she realized he wasn't smiling with her. "So what went wrong?"

"I auditioned three times," he said. "The producers loved me. They said I was amazing. But I was Captain Steele, and there was no way they were going to cast Captain Steele in this sensitive part."

"Type-casting," Gwen murmured.

"Yeah." He sighed again. "I'm tired of that crap, Gwen. I want to make movies like *The Angel* and *Sea Glass*. I know I can do it. But no one will give me the opportunity. To them, I'm just this cartoon character who shoots high-tech weapons and fights with CGI monsters."

"But...you said you blew them away at your audition."

"It doesn't matter. I blew them away, and they all gushed about how perfect I'd be in the role, but the audience would never buy it. In the eyes of the world, I'm Captain Steele. I'll never be anything else."

She processed what he'd just revealed. "What if you stopped making Galaxy Force movies?"

"I'm under contract for the next three films in the series. And—I mean, they pay me well. They treat me well. I feel like a whining bastard, complaining about my career when I'm a freaking movie star. But..." He shrugged. "I'm a little bitter."

"So you decided to leave Hollywood and move to Brogan's Point."

"I wish I could say I came here to be closer to Annie—and to you," he said. "But I didn't even know about Annie. So yeah, I came here because I wanted to get away from all the Hollywood bullshit. I wanted to remember who I was—not Captain Steele but Dylan Scott. Not a star but an actor." He turned toward the TV. "The person I was when I made *Sea Glass*—and when I met you."

She gave his hand a squeeze. "We can watch something else if you'd like."

"No. I want to watch this. With *you*," he added. "Someone who liked me when I was just a guy."

"You're still just a guy," she said. "And I still like you."

He leaned over and kissed the crown of her head. "You're an amazing woman." She turned her face up to his and he touched her lips lightly with his. "Let's watch the movie, amazing woman."

*

"Did you have a sleepover?" Annie asked him the next morning.

He was a little taken aback. When Gwen had invited him to spend the night with her, he couldn't have said no even if he'd wanted to—and he sure as hell hadn't wanted to. In her snug double bed beneath the sloping eaves, they'd made love just as he'd fantasized it, sharing in murmurs what they couldn't shout, in silence what they couldn't murmur. He'd awakened in the early morning, when the sky was pearly with pre-dawn light, and wondered if he should leave before he encountered Annie. But Gwen was asleep, and he couldn't bring himself to wake her up. She worked so hard. She needed her rest.

He'd tiptoed out of the bedroom to take a leak, and when he'd emerged from the bathroom, Annie was waiting for him, dressed in a frill-trimmed flannel nightgown, her hair askew but her eyes wide awake.

"A sleepover?"

"A party where you sleep over. Mike had a sleepover once."

"Did he." Dylan experienced a sharp, unwarranted pang of jealousy.

"He was okay. He never taught me how to play cards, but Mommy said we needed something in our life. I don't remember what it was, but it sounded like something on a farm."

"Pigs?" Dylan guessed.

Annie giggled. "No, silly!: "Something to do with horses. What's that building horses live in?"

"A stable?"

"That's it. Mommy wanted a stable in our life."

"Stability," Dylan guessed.

"Yeah. I don't know why she thought having a sleepover party with Mike would give us a stable."

"Did it bother you that I had a sleepover?" Dylan asked Annie.

She shook her head, "You're nicer than Mike. He never gave me a book. He said he didn't like Legos. He said he stepped on them and they hurt his feet. Will you make me waffles? I like the round kind."

Dylan was momentarily stumped, but then he figured Annie was so smart and so bossy, she'd be able to help him make the waffles. He'd tie her little apron on around her nightie, and they'd be fine.

He followed Annie downstairs to the kitchen, where she showed him the package of waffles in the freezer. Thank goodness he didn't have to make them from scratch. He wondered if Gwen owned a waffle iron.

If she didn't, he'd buy one for his kitchen. If he could have "Squeeze-Pleeze" bottles, he could have a waffle iron.

"Did you like my house?" he asked Annie, once the waffles were in the toaster. He located the cupboard that held the plates and pulled one from the shelf.

"It needs furniture," Annie pointed out. "But it's big."

"How would you feel about living there?"

Seated at the table, Annie kicked her bare legs back and forth while she thought. "Could you put a swing set in the back yard?"

"We could look into it," Dylan said. "The patio takes up a lot of space, but maybe we could find room for a swing set."

"I like the beach," Annie said. "I take swimming lessons."

"It's important for people to know how to swim." The toaster chimed, and he slid two waffles onto a plate for Annie. He recalled having to cut his niece's food for her when she was five, and he cut the waffles into bite-size pieces for Annie. Then he dribbled syrup onto them—not too much, just enough to add flavor. He hoped Gwen would be impressed by his effort. "I have to ask your mother about whether you and she could live in the house. It's up to her."

"She's the mommy," Annie noted, sounding wise beyond her years.

*

The mommy said maybe. She'd looked deeply concerned when she joined Dylan and Annie in the kitchen a few minutes later, her hair mussed and her slender body wrapped in a faded bathrobe held shut by a sash around her waist. The memory of her body was still too fresh in his mind—her taut breasts, the firm curve of her belly, her sleek thighs. He wanted to yank the sash open and haul her into his lap, legs spread wide to welcome him the way she had last night.

Instead, he swallowed a few times, tamping down his lust, and said, "I hope you don't mind. Annie wanted waffles."

"Annie loves waffles," Gwen confirmed, eyeing her daughter cautiously.

"You had a sleepover," Annie said.

"Yes."

"Can I call Dylan Daddy?"

"If he wants you to."

Annie turned to Dylan. "Can I call you Daddy?"

He smiled. He still wanted Gwen, wanted her naked in his arms, pressed against his body. But he realized he'd wanted this at least as much. "Yes," he said. "I'd love for you to call me Daddy."

Chapter Nineteen

Sometimes, Gwen believed she was living in a fairy-tale. Dylan really, seriously, wanted her to move into his mansion by the beach. He requested her input on new appliances for the kitchen, new cabinetry, rugs and lighting fixtures and landscaping around the patio. He spent every evening with her and Annie, and every night with her alone.

"Are you doing this because you feel obligated?" she asked him one night as they sat in the living room, a catalog of plumbing fixtures spread open between them. He wanted to install new vanities in the bathrooms, and decisions had to be made on the basins and faucets.

"Well, the sinks are pretty old," he said. "I want to put in those low-flow toilets, so I might as well put in new sinks, too."

"I mean *me*," Gwen clarified. "Are you including me in your plans because you feel obligated? Because you weren't around for the first five years of Annie's life?"

He set the catalog on the coffee table and arched an arm around her shoulders. "I hate that I wasn't around for those first five years," he admitted. "But no. I wouldn't ask you to share the house with me if I didn't want you to."

"But it's all so...so fast."

"Five years isn't fast."

"We haven't known each other five years."

"Funny." Dylan gave her a sweet, crooked smile. "I feel as if I've known you forever."

"But last time—six years ago—we went our separate ways. We were strangers whose paths had crossed by chance."

"How do any two people meet? Sometimes it's by chance." He stroked his hand through her hair, then sketched a line down her cheek with his fingertips. "We were both on the same wavelength then. We both wanted to go our separate ways. We did what we did and walked away."

That was true. They'd understood each other then. They'd come together because they'd both wanted to, and walked away because they'd both wanted that, too.

And now... She could believe she'd never want to walk away. But she wasn't sure she could believe the same of Dylan.

She loved him. She imagined he had genuine feelings for her, too. But she couldn't get past the fact that he was Captain Steele, a movie star, and she was just plain Gwen Parker, a shop owner and a single mother. If he was staying with her only because of Annie, that would never be enough for her.

"What if you leave?" she asked. "What if you decide you want to walk away again?"

"I won't walk away, Gwen," he vowed. "I'll have to travel sometimes for work. If I'm making a film, I probably won't be able to get home for dinner every night. You go off on location for a few weeks. And there are promotional gigs. Meetings. Press junkets."

"I understand that."

"At least right now, though, we're good. I won't have to go anywhere until we start filming the new Galaxy Force episode. I'd have to check with Brian, but I'm pretty sure I'm scheduled to report to the set on January fifteenth."

That was more than two months away. In two months, she and Dylan could solidify things a bit. Annie could feel secure about her father's presence in her life. They could establish their rhythm, find their groove. Create a family.

Of course, he could go off to the set in January and have an affair with one of the actresses who'd be sharing the screen with him. As Gwen recalled, two actresses in the Galaxy Force were traffic-stopping beautiful.

But a man didn't have to travel to a film set in Hollywood to have an affair. Men had affairs all the time, even if they didn't find themselves in close proximity to breathtakingly gorgeous actresses. Men had affairs even in Brogan's Point.

"I know it's rushing things," he went on, "but if you want to get married, we could do that. I'm thinking it might be good for Annie's sake."

Another woman might consider that proposal lacking in romance. To Gwen, it was the sweetest proposal she could imagine. That he cared so much about Annie made her love him even more.

The thought that he'd suggested marriage out of a sense of obligation troubled her, though. "I don't want a shotgun marriage," she said.

Dylan chuckled. "It's too late for that. You're way beyond pregnant."

Gwen laughed, too. Then she grew somber. "It would be nice if love were a part of it," she said, opting for honesty. "But I was once engaged to be married, and I was crazy in love with the guy, and he left. I don't want to go through that again."

"Then we won't get engaged. Joke," Dylan added. "We can get engaged, we can get married, whatever you want. I like you, Gwen. I think you like me. I can't say we're crazy in love, but the sex is pretty damned great. And we both love Annie. We can make this work."

Definitely not romantic. Yet maybe this was the only kind of marriage that would suit them. They were compatible, and they both wanted what was best for their daughter. And as he said, the sex was pretty damned great. As a basis for marriage, that wasn't bad.

She could only hope that a marriage would create the foundation they needed, the solid ground on which they could build their family. Annie deserved that. She needed it.

Gwen had survived a heartbreak, and she could survive it again. But if this marriage didn't work out and Dylan went away, it would break Annie's heart. And Gwen simply couldn't bear to let that happen.

*

"Are you crazy?" Brian squawked through the phone. "Marriage?"

"She's the mother of my daughter," Dylan said. "Why shouldn't I marry her?"

"Let me count the ways," Brian said. "First of all, it's not like she's some poor, helpless chick. She's been raising the kid on her own for, what, five years? She doesn't need you to step in and make an honest woman out of her."

"True," Dylan conceded. But he'd never considered that he was marrying Gwen to make an honest woman out of her. She already was an honest woman—one of the most honest women he'd ever known. This was the twenty-first century. Unmarried women who had children didn't need the legitimacy of a marriage to make them respectable.

"Second, the tabloids will have a field day. You don't exactly have the reputation of a boy scout, but you come pretty damned close. You've never had a scandal attached to you—which makes the vultures doubly eager to smear you. It's a lot more fun to throw dirt on someone who's clean than on someone who's already dirty."

"I don't see how marrying Gwen would create a scandal."

"Because she's the mother of your child," Brian explained, enunciating each word as if he were addressing an idiot. "Your five-year-old child."

"Not a big thing," Dylan insisted. As long as Gwen and Annie didn't get dragged through the dirt along with him, he wouldn't care what the tabloids said. If necessary, he'd preempt them by arranging a few interviews himself. "I found the love of my life," he'd tell the journalists and talk-show hosts. "I found her, and I lost her, and six years later, I found her again. I'm the luckiest guy in the world."

"Besides," Brian continued, and then listed the names of half a dozen pretty actresses. "All available. All stunning. All interested."

"In me? Doubtful."

"I'm telling you, Dylan—you've got a lot of romantic opportunities here in Tinsel Town. You get married, and you'd be throwing all those opportunities away. Unless you plan to cheat on your wife, which brings us back to the subject of the tabloids."

"I'm not going to cheat on my wife," he said, thinking about how strange the word *wife* felt on his tongue. *Wife.* Could he really go through with this?

He recalled his thoughts about preempting the tabloids by scheduling his own interviews. *I found the love of my life.* Somehow, that thought didn't seem anywhere near as weird as *wife.*

Gwen couldn't possibly be the love of his life, could she?

Why not? She was kind. She was smart. She worked hard, kept her word, devoted herself to her daughter. She was pretty. She was sexy. She asked so little of him—which made him want to give her so much.

"We're not rushing into anything," he promised Brian. "We're just laying the groundwork. But I feel good about it. I think this is the right step to take."

"We'll talk more about this." Brian's statement sounded like a warning. "Let me run it past my partners. If you go through with it, we'll need to find a way to massage your image so it doesn't hurt you."

"It won't hurt me," Dylan said. "I'm a boy scout—your word. Boy scouts get married. Boy Scout values are about honor and responsibility and all."

"Yeah, right," Brian muttered. "Meanwhile, sign a pre-nup. These grand romantic gestures can wind up being seriously expensive."

"I'll think about it," Dylan said, then ended the call, knowing he wouldn't think about it at all. If Gwen had craved his money, she would have gone after him when he was pregnant. She could have hired an attorney. She could have gone to the tabloids herself, or threatened to.

Not once had she acted like a gold-digger.

Joking aside, he was hardly a boy scout. But Gwen... Yeah. She was the very definition of honorable.

Wife. He mouthed the word, whispered it, held it on his tongue. It still felt weird. For some reason, *the love of my life* didn't.

Chapter Twenty

The day after he'd raised the subject of marriage, Dylan checked out of his room at the Ocean Bluff Inn and moved into Gwen's house. The snug little Cape-Cod seemed awfully crowded with him in it, even though his relocation entailed a minimum of clothing and equipment: jeans, shirts, sweaters, his laptop—just whatever he'd fit into his carry-on bags when he'd flown from California to Massachusetts a couple of weeks ago. When his house was ready, he told Gwen that evening as they cleaned the dinner dishes, he'd return to California to move the stuff he had in storage and drive his Porsche back east. "Maybe we can make the trip together with Annie during her school's holiday week at the end of December," he suggested.

"The end of December is a busy time at the store. People have Christmas money to spend."

"Early January, then," Dylan said. "Or I can hire someone to drive the car across the country. Although I'm not sure anyone I hired would treat my baby as well as I do. I love my Porsche." He shot her a quick grin as he scraped the uneaten string beans from Annie's plate into the trash. His smile seemed to acknowledge that *love* wasn't a word he'd used when he'd proposed marriage. "I could arrange to have the moving company put the car in a truck and drive it across the country with my furniture. They'll do that."

Gwen smiled back, although the fact that he could discuss love in the context of his car but not in the context of their marriage sparked a rueful twinge in her chest. She understood the situation. She accepted it. She and Dylan would enter into this marriage with the understanding that it was all about Annie, giving her the security and stability of a two-parent family. As he had said, they could make it work.

Seeing him, a world-famous movie star, scraping plates like a normal human being, made it hard for her not to love him, though. "You're sure you want to do this?" she asked.

"Do what? Help you with the dishes?"

"Move to Brogan's Point. Live with Annie and me."

"I'm sure," he said, giving her shoulder a squeeze. "Don't look so worried. It'll be great."

"Will you even be able to drive your car in New England? Can a souped-up sports coupe handle winter weather?"

"It was built in Germany," he reminded her. "They get snow there."

Have faith, she ordered herself. *Have faith that he'll bring his car to Brogan's Point, that he won't arrive in California, realize he doesn't want to drive in the snow, and decide not to come back.*

He seemed sincere. But he was an actor, Gwen reminded herself. Actors could say anything convincingly. Dylan's entire career was built around getting people to believe he was the commander of an interstellar military force a hundred years in the future. If a viewer could believe that by watching his movies, it was no wonder Gwen could believe him when he said he really wanted to be the father Annie deserved, the father she needed.

Gwen could also believe he wanted her for his wife. Not just his words but his deeds indicated that he was serious about marrying her. She reminded herself that before he was Captain Steele, savior of the universe, he was a small-town boy from Nebraska. No doubt he'd scraped a lot of plates as a kid. He hadn't forgotten how to do mundane chores.

Annie bounced into the kitchen, carrying the book Dylan had given her. "I read one of the poems all by myself," she boasted. "I got most of the words. Can Dylan read the rest to me? I mean, *Daddy*." She was still getting used to the idea.

"Sure," Gwen said, motioning with her head that Dylan should join Annie. "I can finish up here."

"Let me just help your mom with these last few dishes, and then I'll read to you," Dylan promised Annie.

"Can you drive me to swimming tomorrow?" Annie asked him. "I have swimming lessons on Friday after school. Sometimes Mommy has to leave the store to drive me to the community center. But you don't work, so you can drive me instead."

Gwen started to correct Annie, but Dylan was laughing, so she didn't leap to his defense. "I *do* work, Annie," he told her. "But at the moment, I'm between projects. I would consider it an honor to drive you to your swimming class. It'll make your life easier," he added, addressing Gwen.

"We'll need to move Annie's car seat from my car to yours."

"I can't wait until we move her car seat into my Porsche," he said. "Put down the top, tear down Atlantic Avenue... I'll show Annie what a real engine can do."

Gwen grinned and shook her head. "She'll just sit there shouting, 'Faster, faster!'"

The dinner plates done, Gwen waved Dylan and Annie off. Then she settled at the table with a stack of mail. Bills and junk, as usual. Still, it was a luxury to be able to sit quietly after dinner, slitting the envelopes open and perusing their contents without having Annie tugging at her, begging for a story or a game.

She'd rarely thought about how exhausting raising a child alone was. She hadn't allowed herself to think about it. If she had, she would have become depressed or resentful. The last thing she ever wanted was to resent her magnificent daughter.

Just to have a few quiet minutes in the evening could make marrying Dylan worth it. He didn't have to love her. He could aim all his love at his car. But to be able to check her mail before nine o'clock at night? It might not be the most romantic reason to tie the knot, but Gwen would treasure the chance to let someone else take care of Annie for a few precious minutes while she took care of everything else.

She finished sorting the mail, tossed the junk into the recycling bin and slid the bills into neat stack. Then she went off in search of Dylan and Annie.

She found them downstairs in the playroom, cuddled up on the couch with the A.A. Milne book spread open across their laps. A few Mr. Potato-Head pieces lay strewn across the floor, brightly colored plastic lips, an ear, a bowler hat. Dylan read to Annie, his voice low and soothing, with just the right inflections. Of course he would read poetry—even children's verses—beautifully. He'd probably taken a class in poetry reading as part of his acting curriculum.

She hovered at the foot of the stairs, not wanting to interrupt. The scene was so tranquil, a father and daughter sharing a book. *This,* she thought. *This is what marriage to Dylan will be.*

Annie noticed her mother just as Dylan reached the end of the poem. "Dylan's going to take me to swimming," she chirped. "I mean, *Daddy.*"

"I know, honey. I was there when he agreed to do that."

"He'll be the best daddy there. No one else has a daddy taking them to swimming."

"Then I guess I'll be the *only* daddy there," Dylan joked. "Am I supposed to stick around for the entire class?"

"You don't have to," Gwen said. "It lasts about forty-five minutes."

"You could watch if you wanted to," Annie invited him. "We're learning breathing. You blow bubbles with your nose."

"That's pretty exciting," he said, shooting Gwen a wry smile. A jingly bell sounded, and he shifted on the couch to pull his cell phone out of his hip pocket. He eyed the screen, then sighed. "I have to take this call. I'll be right back," he added to Annie, scruffing his fingers through her hair as he stood and lifted the phone to his ear. "Brian? What's up?"

Gwen stepped aside, allowing him to sprint up the stairs as he listened to his caller. She scooped up the scattered bits of Mr. Potato's anatomy and tossed them into their box. Then she settled on the couch next to Annie, who was gazing at the stairs, a moony, dreamy expression on her face. "I like having a daddy," she declared.

"I'm glad he's in our life, too," Gwen told her.

After a minute, Dylan descended the stairs. He looked shell-shocked. "That was Brian," he said.

Gwen wanted to ask him if everything was all right—from his expression, it was hard to tell. But she didn't want to be nosy. Instead, she asked, "Isn't it kind of late to be conducting business?"

"He's in California," Dylan reminded her. "It's three hours earlier there. Gwen... I have to go."

"Go?"

"To L.A. I got the part in *The Angel*."

"What?"

"The director decided the guy they'd hired wasn't working out. They want me. I've got to go."

"When?"

"Now. They need me out there for some rehearsals with the director and the co-stars, and then we'll fly to Toronto for the shoot. If everything times right, I'll be able to have a few days off before I have to start work on the new Galaxy Force movie."

"By now, you mean...tomorrow?"

"Tonight. Brian's arranging a private jet for me. They've already started work on the film. This director likes at least a week of rehearsals before he brings in the cameras. They already had one week with the other actor before dropping him from the project, so they're behind schedule." He must have noticed Gwen's frown, because he added, with a helpless smile, "I'm sorry. But this—you know how much this part means to me."

"Right. Of course," she said, her voice brittle.

"Can you still take me to swimming?" Annie asked, gazing up at him.

He crossed to the sofa and knelt down in front of her. "I'm sorry, Annie. I wish I could. But I've got to go to Los Angeles."

"Where's that?"

"It's far away. About three thousand miles."

Her eyes—those big brown eyes, so much like Dylan's—filled with tears.

"I'm really sorry, Annie."

Sure you are, Gwen thought, anger building inside her. She could take the disappointment. She could take the abandonment. His manager—Brian, the bearer of good news and bad news—had locked her out of Dylan's life years ago, and she'd survived. She'd learned how to be a single mother, how to make ends meet on her own, how to juggle her schedule so she could take her daughter to swim class.

But Annie wasn't so tough. Dylan had wooed her, he'd won her, and now he was leaving her. He'd broken her heart, and Gwen's heart broke for her daughter.

"I guess you'd better go, then," she snapped, her protective-mother instincts rising like a wall between her and the man hunkering down in front of her and her daughter. "Luckily, you don't have much to pack."

Annie turned to Gwen, a few fat tears leaking down her cheeks. "Is he leaving?"

"I'm sorry, Annie," Dylan said for the third time, addressing Annie's hair because she was no longer looking at him. "Remember how you said I wasn't working? Well, it turns out I am working."

"Just go," Gwen ordered him, her voice chilly. She wrapped an arm around Annie and let her daughter nestle into her shoulder, her tears leaving damp spots on her sweater.

Dylan held her gaze for a long moment, then stood and strode towards the stairs. She watched him vanish up them, and the rage that had simmered inside her on Annie's behalf swelled, spreading through her like a wildfire.

At that moment, she hated him. She admitted that her own heartbreak wasn't just for Annie. It was for herself. By wooing Annie, he'd also wooed Gwen. By being attentive, by being affectionate, by letting her believe she finally had a partner with whom to share the joys and challenges of parenthood, by making glorious love to her...

She'd fallen in love with him. And he'd turned and walked away.

Chapter Twenty-One

Landing the starring role in *The Angel* was Dylan's dream-come-true. So why didn't he feel elated?

He sat in the plush leather seat of a Gulfstream that had taken off from a small airport just west of Boston. Brian had scored him a seat and emailed him the *Angel* script, now filling the monitor of his laptop. Dylan tried to focus on the words spread across the glowing screen. He'd memorized the script before he'd auditioned, but now he felt as if he was reading it for the first time. The words seemed alien to him. This role, this character—could he speak these lines? Could he become this person?

Outside the porthole window, the night sky was an inky void. Inside, an attendant wandered among Dylan and the three other businessmen sharing the flight with him, keeping their glasses filled with their drinks of choice—in Dylan's case, a smooth twelve-year-old Glenlivet. He could barely taste it.

Annie's tear-filled eyes were seared into his memory.

So were Gwen's resolutely dry eyes. No tears had filled them. Just a disappointment so deep it seemed bottomless. Disappointment and anger, and bitter resignation.

He wanted this job. It would elevate his career to a new level. It would nourish his creativity. It would stretch him, challenge him, make him sweat in a good, healthy way. Maybe Annie was too young to understand such things, but Gwen wasn't.

This was a major high point in his career—and he felt like shit.

He pulled out his phone, thinking to call her. But it was nearly ten o'clock. The ringing phone might wake up Annie, and possibly Gwen as well. He'd call her tomorrow. He'd call her and swear to her that he did intend to marry her, that he was a man of his word, that he wanted to be a father to Annie.

That Gwen was the love of his life.

How had that happened? How had he fallen in love with her? He wasn't so shallow as to believe he loved her just because they had amazing chemistry in bed. More than chemistry—it was alchemy. Something magical.

That wasn't love, though. That was just fun. Extremely good fun.

Yet when he thought about it, he realized that his decision to marry her was more about what happened out of bed than in it. When he thought about the house he was buying in Brogan's Point, he thought about her in it. He imagined her fussing in the kitchen, leaving her comb and brush and skin lotion in the master bathroom, lounging on the patio—because, damn it, the woman deserved to lounge sometimes. She deserved some time off—from work, from motherhood, from cooking and tidying up and driving Annie to her swimming class. Dylan could picture Gwen on a comfortable, cushioned chair on that lovely patio behind the house, a book in her lap, a glass of wine on a table beside her, and a salty breeze rising from the beach to wreak havoc with her hair.

He thought about her confiding in him—and about him confiding in her. He thought about how easy she was to talk to, how he didn't have to act when he was with her. He didn't have to pretend he cared that some other actor had leapfrogged over him in the Hollywood hierarchy, that some other actor was dating a female star he used to date, and they'd appeared on the cover of *People*, and they were now the "It" couple, the flavor of the week. Brian was always nagging him that these things mattered, and in the world of show-biz, they did. But he'd never been good at pretending he cared, and with Gwen, he didn't have to.

She didn't soar through the galaxy like Captain Steele. She was down-to-earth. He loved that about her.

And she worked so hard, and never complained. After Brian had shut her down and locked her out, she'd soldiered on by herself, doing what needed to be done. No whining. No diva behavior. Just a hard-working, fiercely protective, profoundly loving mother.

Damn. He really, truly loved her.

Finally, he'd achieved an astonishing professional milestone, and he wanted to share it with her. He wanted her on this private jet with him—her and Annie.

Instead, he'd be lucky if she even spoke to him again. He'd promised to marry her, stay with her, live in her sleepy little town and be a father to Annie, and here he was, abandoning her, leaving her as alone as she'd been the day she'd found out she was pregnant. She was probably thinking she'd gotten along without him well enough before, and she could get along without him today.

Just like the song said, he'd turned and walked away. And she hadn't begged him to stay.

Only a fool would want anything to do with him—and Gwen wasn't a fool.

*

He phoned several times over the next few days. Gwen answered the first couple of calls. She talked to him coolly, civilly. He told her about the role in which he'd been cast, explained to her how much this film could mean for his career, reminded her that one reason he'd decided to move to Brogan's Point was because filmmakers were so determined to type-cast him as an action-adventure comic-book hero, and he'd wanted to escape from all that. But now, at last, a filmmaker decided he was capable of more.

So you don't need to live in Brogan's Point, she'd thought.

"It's an amazing opportunity," Dylan had insisted. "At this point, I can't afford to turn down something that could open so many more doors for me."

"I'm not judging you," Gwen had assured him. "This is your choice. It's a good choice for you."

"But not for you," he'd said.

She'd been touched that he cared enough to consider the situation from her perspective. Most men weren't that sensitive. "I'm no worse off than I was before you showed up, Dylan," she'd said, even though that wasn't entirely true. Before he'd showed up, she hadn't been in love with him. She'd been contemplating marrying Steve in order to provide her daughter with a two-parent home.

She wouldn't go back to Steve now. One thing Dylan had done for her, besides making her fall in love with him, was to force her to recognize that marrying someone just to provide her daughter with a father wasn't right.

Annie had a father. He was currently three thousand miles away. If Gwen needed child support, she knew he'd provide it. In another twelve years, if Annie wanted to go to college, Gwen would send Dylan the tuition bills. Who knew? Maybe by then, the Attic would be a national chain, like Target or Wal-Mart, and she'd be Annie's wealthy parent. Anything was possible.

Annie wanted to know where her father was. "He had to leave," Gwen told her. "He had to go back to California for his job."

"Why can't he have a job here?" Annie asked.

"Things don't always work out the way we want them to," Gwen said, which seemed like a pretty painful lesson for Annie to have to learn at such a tender age. She thought about letting Annie speak to Dylan when he phoned, but opted not to. For one thing, he might think Gwen was trying to guilt-trip him by forcing him to listen to Annie's painful questions. For another, Gwen didn't want to give Annie any reason to think Dylan might return. He'd had his chance to plant his roots in Brogan's Point. He'd probably believed he would actually do that. It must have seemed like a great idea—until Hollywood had crooked her tempting finger at him, and he'd gone running back to her.

At least Gwen hadn't confided to Diana or her other friends about his proposal. They would have hated him for ditching her so soon after he'd asked her to marry him.

Gwen didn't want to hate him. How could she hate the man who'd given her Annie?

She hoped that in time, she could stop loving him. She hoped she could forgive him for walking out of her life not once but twice. She was a big girl, strong and independent. *Old enough to face the dawn.* Wasn't that what the song had said?

He wanted to be the angel. And here she was, an angel of the morning. Walking away. In time, she promised herself—in time it wouldn't hurt so much.

*

On Friday, she left the store at three-thirty to pick up Annie at her after-school program and get her to the community center for her four o'clock swim class. The air was cold and crisp, pumpkins and gourds displayed on porches and in windows, ghosts constructed of old sheets dangling from trees. She and her staff had adorned the front window of the Attic with fake cobwebs, plastic skeletons, and ceramic jack-o-lanterns. Annie's dinnertime conversation had gradually evolved from "Where's my daddy?" to "Can I be a magic kite for Halloween?"

"I thought you wanted to be a princess," Gwen reminded her last night.

"Lucy and Cara are going to be princesses. I want to be something different. I could be a kite, and Mr. Snuffy can be Maggie, the girl who rides on the kite. Can we do that?"

It sounded awfully creative to Gwen, and a lot more original than the princess costume they'd discussed earlier that month. "I think we can rig something up," she said. A couple of lightweight slats glued into a cross, with fabric stretched over them and a little tail of knotted rags attached... Annie would look adorable as she trick-or-treated.

Gwen arrived at Annie's elementary school and entered the art room, where the after-school program for the younger children was located. A dozen other children were busy painting with watercolors, instructed by that red-haired art teacher—Monica's friend Emma. Gwen recalled Annie mentioning that Emma came now and then to lead art classes in the program.

She scanned the room but didn't see Annie.

Anxious, she approached Emma. "I'm supposed to pick up my daughter, Annie Parker. Is she in one of the other rooms?"

Wiping her hands on a towel, Emma frowned. "She left ten minutes ago."

"She did?" Gwen's heart beat harder. "How? Who was she with?"

"Her father."

That couldn't be. Annie's father was in California, or maybe Toronto, or wherever he was, starring in this wonderful dream-come-true movie. "She left with a man? What man? He wasn't her father!"

"She said he was. She raced to him and screamed, 'Daddy!' and he gave her a big hug. I was a little startled, because he looked a lot like that actor in the Galaxy Force movies—except his hair was a lot longer and he had a stubble of beard. He was wearing a shabby leather jacket and jeans. But cut his hair and put him in Spandex, and I swear he could pass for that actor...what's his name? Dylan Scott, right?"

Gwen's pulse slowed, but only slightly. If Annie was with Dylan, she was probably safe. But where would he take her? When Gwen had seen Dylan at the Faulk Street Tavern a few weeks ago, her first fear was that he'd discover Annie's existence and try to take her away from Gwen. Now that fear reared up inside her. Had he spirited Annie off to Los Angeles in a fancy private jet? Or to the movie set? Or...

"He said he was going to take her to the community center, and Annie said that was what he'd promised."

"Okay." Gwen took a few deep breaths and ordered herself to remain calm. She thanked Emma, and resolved to discuss lax security with the program director once she'd found Annie and made sure she was okay. She supposed Emma couldn't really be blamed for allowing Annie to leave with Dylan. Annie had identified him as her father—which he was. Emma didn't know better.

Gwen left the building, tightening her scarf around her throat to ward off the chilly autumn breeze, and drove to the community center. Had Dylan strapped Annie into a proper car seat? Did he even know what a proper car seat for a five-year-old girl was?

At the community center, Gwen raced down the hall, following the scent of chlorine to the pool. She swept inside and the warm, humid air wrapped around her, nearly suffocating her. Scanning the room, she spotted several parents seated on the bleachers flanking the pool.

When Gwen took Annie to this class, she couldn't stay and watch her daughter. She always had to race back to the store, and then come back an hour later to pick Annie up and help her out of her wet swimsuit.

Some of the other mothers did stay to watch the class, though. And today, one father was also watching.

Gwen unwrapped her scarf, unbuttoned her jacket and picked her way carefully over the damp tiles to the bleachers. She cast a glance at the students, who were making their way across the width of the pool, clinging to kickboards and turning the water foamy white with their vigorous kicking. Despite the splashing and shrieking, Gwen had no trouble picking Annie out of the crowd, creating a wild wake of splashing bubbles with her feet.

Gwen reached the bleachers and climbed to Dylan's bench. He saw her and rose, a tentative smile curving his beautiful mouth. He had removed his jacket, and she tried not to admire the snug fit of his sweater, tried not to remember the hunky male chest beneath it. "Hey," he said when she reached him. He lifted his arms as if to hug her, then let them fall back to his sides, apparently unsure whether she'd welcome a hug.

"What are you doing here?"

"I told Annie I'd take her to her swimming class. And here I am."

"But..." Gwen scowled and shook her head. Dylan gestured toward the bench. Given how dazed she felt, she decided she'd better sit. "You're making your movie."

"I'm trying to do both. We filmed until ten this morning, and then I hopped on a plane and got here just in time."

"From California?"

"Toronto. It's a quick flight. Under two hours."

"By private jet," she guessed.

He shrugged. "This was important."

It *was* important—not the swimming class as much as Dylan's promise to bring Annie to it. But his movie was important, too. He'd said it was an amazing opportunity.

"I asked the director to work with me. It turns out he'd always wanted me for the part, and the money guys were the ones who'd vetoed me. He's willing to be flexible. I told him I had a daughter in Massachusetts, and I wanted to spend as much time here as I could. So he's scheduled my scenes so that I can leave the set Friday afternoons. I'll have to be back Sunday night, though."

Gwen's mind snagged on the word *daughter*. "You told him about Annie?"

"Yeah. I'm sorry. I hope it doesn't backfire. But...yeah."

"Why would it backfire?"

"Well, the tabloids, the gossip. I don't know. We'll have to figure out a way to protect her from their prying eyes." He inched slightly closer to Gwen on the bench, his thigh barely touching hers. "Annie's not the only reason I came back," he said, his dark gaze locking with hers, his eyes like hot chocolate, dark and steamy.

"Your house," she said, afraid to read too much into his intense stare.

He chuckled. "That, too." He sighed, bowed his head, and touched his lips lightly to hers. "You, Gwen. I came back for you."

They were the words she'd longed to hear. The words she'd refused to admit she longed to hear.

"We'll figure this out," he said, his voice low, a hushed contrast to the shrieks and giggles of the children, echoing off the hard tile surfaces of the room. "I said we would, and I meant it. I'll have to travel sometimes. I can't help that. If possible, I'll bring you and Annie with me. If you can't leave the store, I'll understand. But...we're family, Gwen. I've missed out on the first five years of this family, and I don't want to miss out anymore."

So it *was* about Annie. That was okay. Gwen would accept that.

"As soon as I got on that plane to California, I realized I didn't want to go. I wanted the part—God, you can't imagine how much I wanted it. But I want you, too."

"Annie, you mean."

"No. I mean you. I love you, Gwen." He reached behind him for his jacket, dug his hand into a pocket, and pulled out a small velvet box. "Let's do this right. Marry me, Gwen."

He handed her the box, and she opened it with trembling fingers. Inside was the most beautiful ring she'd ever seen, white gold with an oval diamond solitaire surrounded by tiny diamond chips. "I had my mother express this to me. It was my grandmother's. Your family names girls after grandmothers. My family goes with heirloom rings."

"So you told your family about me?"

"About you and Annie. They can't wait to meet you. I know you've got the store and everything, but I was thinking, maybe we could fly them here for Thanksgiving. Your parents, too. I don't know if we can get the house ready in time, but I can book a bunch of rooms at the Ocean Bluff Inn and we can have a big Thanksgiving party."

It all seemed so homey. So unglamorous, so un-Hollywood.

So Dylan.

"Yes," she said.

"You like that idea? A Thanksgiving gathering at the Ocean Bluff Inn?"

"Yes, I'll marry you." She pulled the ring from its slot and slid it onto her finger. The overhead fluorescent light caught its facets, making it glitter as if lit by an inner fire. "Yes," she murmured, pulling Dylan in for another kiss. Not as deep a kiss as she would have liked—they were at the community center pool, after all—but one that conveyed how very much she loved him, how very happy she was.

"No more walking away," he whispered once the kiss ended.

She smiled, her lips so close to his, she was sure he could feel her smile against them. "No more walking away," she vowed.

***

About the Author

Judith Arnold is the award-winning, bestselling author of more than one hundred published novels. A New York native, she currently lives in New England, where she indulges in her passions for jogging, dark chocolate, good music, good wine and good books. She is married and the mother of two sons.

For more information about Judith, or to contact her, please visit her website[1]. Feel free to check out her other books[2] and sign up for her newsletter[3].

If you enjoyed *Angel of the Morning*, I hope you will consider posting a review of it online. Thank you!

Here's a preview of *Rescue Me*, Book Eight in the Magic Jukebox series:

Sam Harper couldn't sleep. It was too damned quiet.

It was also eight-thirty in the evening, ridiculously early for any self-respecting man to be in bed alone. But yesterday he'd pulled a night shift that had wound up running eleven hours. A couple of inches of fresh snow had made the roads slick, and he'd had to deal with four car accidents, one serious enough to require an ambulance. No deaths, thank God. Nothing tragic. Just a lot of fear and anger, aches and pains. And paperwork. Tons of paperwork. Even if most of it was done on computers and didn't entail actual paper... Bureaucracy was bureaucracy.

When you were the new kid in town, you had to expect to get stuck with snowy night shifts. Sam wouldn't complain. He was grateful that the Brogan's Point Police Department had taken him on when he'd needed to get the hell out of New York.

---

1.   http://www.juditharnold.com/

2.   http://www.juditharnold.com/book-store/

3.   http://mad.ly/signups/60624/join

The lack of noise here freaked him out, though. He lay in his bed, in a third-floor walk-up a couple of blocks from the ocean, listening to the nothingness beyond his windows. Back in New York, he would have been lulled to sleep by a symphony of street sounds: buses wheezing along Broadway, the IRT train rattling over the bridge into the Bronx, inebriated people shouting at one another, the pulsing bleat of a car alarm in the distance, the wail of a siren. You got used to it, so used to it that trying to fall asleep in a quiet town perched on the ocean's edge north of Boston was impossible.

He stared into the surrounding dark, wondering how long he ought to stay where he was, pretending sleep would settle onto him like a thick winter quilt if he just remained motionless. But his stillness only emphasized the stillness beyond his building's walls. A car cruised down the street outside his window, a whisper of tires against the slushy pavement, fading to silence as the vehicle turned the corner and drove away

In the kitchen, the refrigerator motor hummed.

Time to face the ugly truth: Sam wasn't going to fall asleep.

He pushed himself to sit, raked his hand through his hair, and reached for the jeans he had tossed over the back of the chair a few feet from his bed. He stood, pulled on a T-shirt and over it a sweater, and stuffed his feet into thick wool socks. Wallet, phone, and keys in his pockets, he strode out of the bedroom. His boots stood drying on yesterday's newspaper near the door. He laced them on, grabbed his jacket from the coat tree, and headed out into the chilly January night. Maybe a walk would tire him out.

The icy air chafed his cheeks. Despite the ocean's proximity, Brogan's Point was much drier than Manhattan. The wintry atmosphere reminded him of the chilled martinis Maggie used to enjoy in Callahan's after a shift. She'd always stay for one drink, then go home to her husband. One drink was okay with Sam, just enough to decompress.

He wasn't into cocktails. He usually opted for beer. Maggie had been a martini aficionado, an expert, highly opinionated on the pluses and minuses of various garnishes—olive versus onion versus lemon peel. She'd insist that he taste her drink as she tried to educate him about the nuances of this or that brand of vodka. He could never detect any difference, though. They all tasted the same to him: not as good as beer.

Thoughts of Maggie made his head swim and his shoulders seize. He shrugged to loosen them, swallowed hard, and headed in the direction of Atlantic Avenue and the beach beyond the sea wall.

Stupid decision. The bitter wind coming off the water slammed into him. He walked faster, his hands shoved into the pockets of his jacket. He should have worn gloves. They weren't doing him any good sitting on the kitchen counter.

Should've worn a scarf, too. Should've worn a hat. Should've stayed home and banged his head against a wall until he knocked himself unconscious.

He turned up the collar of his jacket and hunched against the frigid sea breeze. To his left, the ocean was a stretch of black, meeting a black sky at an invisible horizon.

No moon tonight, but the streetlights illuminated Atlantic Avenue well enough. Cars drove up and down the road, which had been salted and plowed, leaving fringes of dirty snow along the curb. He supposed that in Brogan's Point, this much traffic would be considered just a few vehicles short of rush hour. But you wouldn't have to say a prayer before trying to cross the street here. So different from New York City, where cars and cabs, trucks and buses barreled down the avenues and sped along the cross-streets, slowing for a red light only if they had no alternative.

Well, he'd wanted *so different from New York City*. He'd needed *so different from New York City*. His hope was that once he was better, once the nightmares ended, he'd return to the noise and the crowds and the turmoil and energy of the Big Apple. Maybe in a year. Maybe sooner.

Another blast of ocean air smacked into him, making him shiver. He noticed an illuminated sign a short distance up a side street: Faulk Street Tavern. It beckoned to him. Some warmth, a beer—or a cold, dry martini, a toast to Maggie—might buff the rough edges off his nerves. He turned the corner, his long strides carrying him to the door and inside.

Ah. Warmth. The pub was heated not just by a furnace but by bodies, by chatter and laughter and gentle amber lighting. The Faulk Street Tavern appeared to be an unpretentious place—scuffed tables, scuffed linoleum flooring with a scuffed wood dance floor surrounded on one side by booths, on another by free-standing tables, on a third by an ancient-looking jukebox and a sign reading "Restrooms," with an arrow pointing down a back hall, and on the fourth by a long bar lined with stools, most of them occupied. Most of the tables were occupied, too. Servers in white shirts and black pants meandered through the room, carrying trays filled with pitchers and mugs, stemware glasses, and platters of wings or flatbread pizzas or nachos drowning in melted cheese.

Sam surveyed the room and spotted a familiar face at the bar. Ed Nolan, a detective on the Brogan's Point police force, was perched on a stool, angled so that Sam could see only part of his profile. He recognized Ed's build, his broad shoulders, square jaw and salt-and-pepper hair, the khaki trousers and thick-soled leather shoes he'd had on that morning, when he'd entered the squad room and found Sam hunched over his computer, typing up his final accident report of the night. Ed had advocated for Sam when Sam had been desperate to find a new job. Although Sam had completed detective training in New York, he'd wound up leaving the NYPD before he could receive his promotion. Ed had argued that Brogan's Point needed another detective on its force. He'd thrown Sam a lifeline, and Sam had grabbed it and held on tight.

What he'd learned, in the few weeks since he'd joined the local squad, was that detectives in a small town had to be flexible. They had to fill in as patrol officers, manage their own paperwork, and handle fender-benders on winter nights when the roads were treacherous. "We all do whatever's got to be done," Ed had explained to him.

Sam hadn't taken Ed for a heavy drinker, and as he crossed the room to the bar, he saw a plain porcelain mug planted on the bar in front of the guy. Could be coffee laced with something, or just straight-up coffee. Sam would bet on the second option.

"Hey, Sam," Ed greeted him, stretching one long arm out to snag an unoccupied stool and dragging it closer to his own. "I thought you'd be dead to the world by now, after your last shift."

"I thought I'd be dead to the world, too." Sam shrugged. "Instead, here I am."

"In that case, welcome to the Faulk Street Tavern." Ed signaled to the bartender, a tall middle-aged woman with short tufts of rust-colored hair framing her face. "Gus, this is Sam Harper, the police department's new acquisition. Sam, Augusta Naukonen, the owner of this fine establishment. What are you drinking?"

"I'll have a beer, thanks," Sam said, turning to Ms. Naukonen. "Whatever you've got on tap."

She smiled and pulled a clean glass from a shelf. Sam reached for his wallet, but Ed nudged Sam's hand away from his hip pocket before he could pull the wallet out. "On me," he said.

"Thanks." Sam knew better than to argue with Ed about who would pay for his beer.

"I've got a running tab," Ed explained.

The bartender snorted a laugh. "Running for how many years now?"

"She's my girlfriend," Ed told Sam. "She'll be my wife once she realizes resistance is futile."

That got an even bigger laugh out of her. She set the glass of beer on a cocktail napkin in front of Sam and gave Ed's arm a poke. "If you'll excuse me, I've got more important people to take care of." She shot Sam a grin, then strode down the bar to fill an order from one of the servers.

"If you're going to have a girlfriend, a bar owner isn't a bad choice," Sam said.

Ed grinned.

Sam took a sip of beer, then swiveled on his stool so he could gaze out at the room. Partly it was a cop's instinct—always check out your surroundings, searching for any signs of incipient trouble. Partly it was just plain curiosity.

A couple of women wearing black bomber jackets, skinny jeans, and too much make-up hovered near the jukebox. A quartet of burly men at one of the tables made a big show of divvying up a flatbread pizza, cheerfully accusing one another of being greedy pigs. Two women sat facing each other at the booth nearest the bar, drinking wine and talking. The one with her back to Sam had hair so bright a red, it almost looked as if her scalp was on fire. The other one had dark blond hair, long and wavy. Her features were delicate and her posture was unusually straight. He wondered if she had a back injury and was wearing a brace.

No, she wasn't. She looked too slim, her gray sweater hugging the slender curves of her torso. He saw no odd bulges that would indicate there was anything under that sweater besides her body.

Music suddenly blasted from the jukebox, a lively, bouncy tune that sounded vaguely familiar to Sam. A Beatles song, he recognized. His mother was a big Beatles fan. She had all their music on vinyl albums from her childhood, and on CD's she'd acquired more recently so she could listen to them today, decades after she'd last owned a turntable.

A bunch of patrons leaped to their feet, crowding the dance floor. "What's with the ancient music?" Sam asked Ed.

"It's that jukebox," Ed told him. "It only plays oldies."

"It looks pretty old itself."

"According to local legend, the jukebox was standing here before the Faulk Street Tavern even existed. They built the place around it. Right, Gus?" he called to the bartender, who had apparently been eavesdropping on their conversation while she shook, stirred, and poured cocktails.

"Not legend," she said. "It's the truth."

Sam chuckled. "So it plays Beatles music?"

"It plays whatever it wants," Ed answered.

"Only if you put a quarter in it," Gus added as she passed the drinks over the bar to one of the waitresses. "Three songs for a quarter. One song for a dime, but no one ever puts in just a dime."

"And it plays whatever it wants?" That didn't make sense to Sam. Surely the person who inserted the coin could press the buttons and select the songs.

Ed must have read his confusion in his face. "You can't pick the songs. You put in a quarter and it plays three songs. You never know what's going to come out of it."

Weird. But the jukebox was beautiful, a bullet-shaped sculpture of polished wood, with stained-glass peacocks adorning the sound panel in front. "If you say so."

"Sometimes a song will cast a spell," the bartender added. "Be careful. You could wind up bewitched."

Okay. That was beyond weird. Sam didn't believe in magic. He was from New York. New Yorkers were by nature cynical and skeptical. They didn't believe anything, even if it was just inches from their eyes, complete with charts and graphs and explanatory text written by some scholar with a Ph.D.

The folks dancing didn't seem to be under a spell. They were just having a rowdy good time—a much better time than Sam had been having in his apartment, listening to the silence around him. There was plenty enough noise here. Happy noise.

The redhead and the blonde in the booth near him slid out of their seats and joined the dancers. A lesbian couple? he wondered as he watched them dance. The redhead bounced around in a giddy frenzy. The blonde moved more smoothly, more gracefully, her limbs uncannily flexible.

An erotic image flashed through Sam's mind: the two of them, in bed with him. Bouncy, graceful, and him sandwiched in between.

Shame on him. He took a sip of his beer and laughed at his crude male instincts.

The Beatles song ended and another song began. He didn't recognize this one at all. A woman's voice, loud and lusty, begged for someone to rescue her. She was lonely. She was blue. She needed love.

The blonde said something to the red-head, who shook her head and returned to the table. The blonde remained on the dance floor, dancing by herself.

Nothing remarkable about that, Sam told himself. Lots of people danced by themselves, especially when a dance floor was crowded enough to absorb them. Sam wasn't much of a dancer—he always felt self-conscious, unsure of what to do with his limbs—but he'd been at a few gatherings where everyone danced with everyone in one big, sweaty mob. Usually those gatherings involved the consumption of copious quantities of alcohol. But hey, this was a bar. Alcohol consumption was what it was all about.

The woman didn't appear drunk, however. She was poised and elegant, her arms gliding through the air, her hips swaying back and forth, her body moving so fluidly she made all the other dancers sharing the dance floor with her look clumsy and clunky. Sam could watch her dance all day. All night. She moved as if she owned the song, owned the bar, owned the world.

Her gaze locked with his, and for a strange moment, he could have sworn she was dancing only for him. He could have sworn he was on that dance floor with her, one of the clumsy, clunky ones, while she wove magic around him and the singer soulfully pleaded to be rescued. He could have sworn he was enchanted—by the dancer, by the song. By *something.*

Wait. No. Sam didn't believe in magic.

He tried to swivel away, to break the spell that seemed to wrap around him and the willowy woman. Whatever he was feeling, it wasn't magic. Ed's bar-owner girlfriend had simply planted a silly idea in Sam's mind, and he'd proven susceptible to it because...

Because he was tired. Yeah, that sounded like a plausible explanation. He was tired and drained, his mental abilities sluggish. He should be back at his apartment, sound asleep.

Instead, he was in this pub, sipping a beer, listening to a singer belt out a song and watching a beautiful woman dance for him.

She wasn't dancing for him. Not really.

But damn.

Seeing her almost made him believe in magic. Almost.

*

By the time the song ended, Cali's entire body felt as if it had lost its substance. It was movement, motion, energy. What was that Einstein equation? $E=MC^2$. Mass could be converted to energy, right?

Sure—if it was moving at the speed of light squared.

Her body wasn't moving particularly fast. Her mind wasn't moving at all. She'd slid into a zone, something she was skilled at, a place where thought vanished and sweet emptiness took over, a oneness with her surroundings. Right now, she felt a oneness with the song. *Come on, baby, and rescue me.*

And a oneness with that man at the bar. She'd never seen him before, which was a shame, because he was awfully good-looking. His hair was dark, a bit shorter than it ought to be but adorably tousled. His eyes were dark, too, with a sexy sleepiness about them, and his jaw was darkened with a shadow of beard. His jacket hung open, revealing a lean, strong torso. His faded jeans hugged long legs. He had an athlete's build, not muscle-bound but sleek and agile. She'd love to see him doing a warrior pose, or a plank, radiating strength and energy.

He was watching her. His gaze was so intense, she could almost feel it like a caress. It embraced her. She sensed it wrapping around her, exerting a strange pressure on her. His gaze and the song: *Come on, baby, and rescue me.*

I don't need to be rescued, she thought—and then she thought some more. *Maybe I do.*

The song ended and the man turned away. Cali eased back into reality, becoming aware of the din of voices in the tavern, the clatter of glasses and dishes, the smell of liquor scenting the air. She no longer felt as if her spirit had turned into music, as if her body was a physics equation, as if there was no other world except the world of the song...and that man, who clearly had about as much interest in rescuing her as she had in being rescued. Which was no interest at all.

A third song began, slow and moody. A few couples took over the dance floor, arms wrapped tightly around each other, bodies pressed together so intimately that one of those loud-mouth jackasses who had minutes ago been arguing over how to divvy up the table's pizza shouted, "Get a room!" The dancers ignored him.

Cali returned to the table where Emma waited for her, wine glass in hand and eyes glittering with amusement, Cali's gaze snagged on the man at the bar. Even though he wasn't looking at her, she felt something connecting them, an invisible thread pulled taut between them.

Yeah, right. What she felt was the healthy interest of a woman checking out a really hot guy. He might have watched her while she danced, but he was done with her now.

She slid onto the banquette across from Emma and reached for her glass. "God, you dance so beautifully," Emma said. "I can't believe you never took ballet."

Cali shook her head and laughed. "Who needs ballet when you've been doing yoga since you cut your first tooth?"

"I should sign up for one of your classes," Emma said. "Maybe when my life calms down."

"Life never calms down," Cali reminded her. "Except for when you're doing yoga. Yoga makes it calm down."

"See? You should be teaching this at the community center." Emma leaned forward. "Just talk to Nick Fiore. I'm sure he'd love to give you space to teach a beginner's class there. Look what he did for me."

Emma was a painter. Nick Fiore, who coordinated programs at the Brogan's Point Community Center, had hired her to teach an art class there. According to her—and to some of Cali's students at the Body Shop—the class was wonderful.

Cali had no interest in enrolling in Emma's class. She had no artistic talent. But when she'd decided she needed a whimsical mural to brighten up the children's room at the Body Shop, she'd commissioned Emma for the job. Emma had created an amazing wall, featuring flowers exploding with color and animals grinning and cavorting. The kids who spent time in the children's room while their parents worked out in the main studio seemed to love the mural.

Cali certainly loved it. She also loved making a new friend. By the time Emma had finished painting the wall, she and Cali had forged a sisterly bond.

When Emma had phoned her a few hours ago and suggested they go out for drinks, Cali hadn't had to think for more than a few seconds. "Will Max be joining us?" she'd asked. Max was Emma's fiancé. As a couple, they were living proof that opposites attracted: an abundantly talented painter and a hard-wired computer geek. They were a great couple, though. Cali sometimes wondered whether she ought to stop dating guys like herself and find an opposite to fall in love with.

The only problem was, she had no idea what her opposite might be.

That, and she'd rather not fall in love. Not when some secret admirer was so in love with her he was freaking her out.

"I'm telling you," Emma said, "teaching at the community center gave my career such a boost. The connections I've made... Like you! You heard about me through the community center, and you hired me."

"Yes, but you didn't have an established business," Cali pointed out. "You were new in town, giving private art lessons and taking any commissions you could find. I've got the Body Shop. It's been open for three years. I teach classes there. I run programs. I don't need to be teaching classes and running programs at the community center, too."

"Not classes and programs. One class. The publicity would be priceless."

"I advertise." Cali shrugged. She was making a decent living with the Body Shop. She didn't need more. "If I taught a class at the community center, I'd be cannibalizing my own business. People would say, 'Why should I sign up for classes at the Body Shop when I can take classes at the community center?'"

Emma shook her head. "Different audience. Different customers. The people who would take your class at the community center are people who'd never take any classes at the Body Shop—until they took that community center class and discovered they wanted to keep going, sign up for intermediate and advanced classes, maybe a taekwondo class or something. And you could charge the same amount for the community center class as you do for your Body Shop class, so you wouldn't be losing any money."

Her argument made sense. "I'll think about it," Cali promised. She *would* think about it—once she stopped thinking about the stupid messages from her obnoxious lover-boy.

Her gaze strayed from Emma to the bar. The man with the mussed dark hair and the bedroom eyes was still planted on his stool, chatting with an older man who held a coffee mug in his hand. The younger guy stroked his fingers over his stubbly jaw and glanced in Cali's direction.

His gaze held her captive. *Rescue me,* she thought, although she couldn't tell whether she was pleading for him to rescue her, or fearing that he was the one she needed rescuing from.

***

Rescue Me—available now!

Don't miss the other books in the Magic Jukebox series:

Changes

Antiques dealer Diana Simms is engaged to her longtime boyfriend when she finds herself inside the Faulk Street Tavern. The song "Changes" emerges from the jukebox and casts its spell on her. It also captivates Nick Fiore, a local boy who's arrived at adulthood the hard way, after a tour through the juvenile justice system. Now he's dedicated his life to helping other troubled kids. He has no business even looking at a beautiful, well-bred woman wearing a diamond engagement ring. But once they're bewitched by the jukebox, he and Diana must change their lives, their goals, their dreams and their hearts.

True Colors

When she finds herself homeless, artist Emma Glendon accepts the invitation of her best friend to share a rental house in Brogan's Point. But their absentee landlord, Nick Tarloff, has come to town from his home in San Francisco to sell the house, which will mean evicting his tenants. Nick is a high-tech brainiac and a self-made millionnaire. Emma is a painter and a free spirit. They have nothing in common—except the jukebox, which plays "True Colors" and forces them to recognize their own true colors, colors that can match and blend magnificently, if the magic of the jukebox has its way.

Wild Thing

Monica Reinhart is a good girl. A hometown girl. After college, she returned to Brogan's Point to help run the family business, an oceanfront inn. She's never done a wild thing in her life. When Ty Cronin sails into town, his wildness intrigues her. When the jukebox plays "Wild Thing," that wildness infects her, and soon she finds herself doing things she never would have imagined. But Ty could be big trouble. She hardly knows him. She mustn't trust him. Yet once she's taken a walk on the wild side with him, how can she go back to being a good hometown girl?

Heat Wave

Caleb Solomon's office air conditioner is on the fritz. Although not his choice, he winds up meeting with a difficult but profitable client in the pleasant chill of the air-conditioned Faulk Street Tavern. It's there that high school teacher Meredith Benoit finds him. Due to a silly prank, her job and her reputation are in jeopardy. She needs a lawyer, fast. But the Magic Jukebox starts playing "Heat Wave," and a hot wave of passion crashes over Caleb and Meredith, catching them in its undertow and carrying them off.

Moondance

Cory Malone and Talia Roszik married as teenagers after Talia became pregnant. Their marriage didn't last, but their love for their daughter did. Fifteen years after their divorce, Wendy Malone is graduating from high school, and Cory has traveled to Brogan's Point for the occasion. But Cory's and Talia's plans—and their emotions—are thrown into turmoil when they hear the Magic Jukebox play "Moondance." Can a single song make them forget all the hurt and rediscover the love that once brought them together?

Take the Long Way Home

Maeve Nolan left Brogan's Point ten years ago in anger and pain, planning never to return. She hadn't known that Harry, her sweet, silver-haired friend, was a billionaire, but her unexpected inheritance from him lures her back to town. If she's going to remain, she will have to mend her tattered relationship with her father, Police Detective Ed Nolan, and his girlfriend, Gus Naukonen—the owner of the Faulk Street Tavern. She'll also have to deal with Quinn Connor, Brogan's Point's one-time golden boy, who's changed his life but can't escape the expectations the folks in town have of him. When the tavern's Magic Jukebox plays "Take the Long Way Home," it casts its spell on Maeve and Quinn. Can they find home in each other's arms?

CPSIA information can be obtained
at www.ICGtesting.com
Printed in the USA
BVHW031451170119
538098BV00001B/12/P